Novel Slices

Issue Seven

Front Cover
Photo by Max Pasko
Totality in Denton, TX

Back Cover
Photo by Hardy Griffin
Totality in Henderson, NY

> Issues are $15 each for the print version
>
> (free shipping in the US) or
>
> $10 digital (EPUB & PDF versions)
>
> See our website for more info:
>
> www.novelslices.com/issues

Since 2020, *Novel Slices* has published 5 novel excerpt winners per issue and has helped many promising writers obtain literary representation and/or publication.

Novel Slices is a member of the Community of Literary Magazines and Presses (CLMP) and follows their contest code of ethics. The copyright for each excerpt reverts immediately after publication to the author.

Contest Judge	Juliette Wade
Founding Editor	Hardy Griffin
Editor	Stephanie Johnson
Associate Editors	Maria Picone
	Mandy Munro
	Jenna Goodman

All five excerpts in this issue are equal first-place winners in the Novel Slices contest. The editors have chosen the order here solely for the flow of subjects and styles.

Table of Contents

Editor's Note	1
Bitter Orange Rum by Ony Ratsifandrihamanana	2
The Hoard: A Novel of Disordered Family by Sean Gill	19
Nat & Z by Olivia Strauss	35
Great Dismal Swamp by Faith Shearin	56
The Path of the Sun by Lauren Goodsmith	73
Biographies	85
Contest Finalists	87

Editor's Note

Lucky Issue #7! Many of the excerpts in this issue seem to be in conversation with other works, and yet each offers a much-needed update.

For instance, *Bitter Orange Rum* felt uncannily to me as I read it like a number of Gabriel García Márquez's works, but now focusing on how national politics in Madagascar play out in one woman's struggle to give birth.

Then, the way objects become profound metaphors in *The Hoard* is delightfully reminiscent of Tim O'Brien's *The Things They Carried*, although in this excerpt we are not at war (as such) but rather delving deep into the cat's cradle of relationships in a family.

Nat & Z is very much its own beautiful drama of what it means to be young in that teenage moment when everything goes from just hanging out to the intricate and confusing rise of sexual attraction. At the same time, I found myself thinking 'this is *The Catcher in the Rye* we need now.'

Maris, the twelve-year-old girl who narrates *Great Dismal Swamp*, moves with her mother and brother to Ocracoke Island in North Carolina—this turns out to be my version of paradise, as Maris works at the family bookstore and has dreams where Blackbeard is a disembodied hero.

Last but far from least, we find ourselves in Mauritania on the edge of the Western Sahara in *The Path of the Sun*. I had no idea I'd been waiting years for a new and better version of Paul Bowles and Paul Theroux! A woman who has come to see her friend gets a brief, intense taste of the lives of refugees of a war most people may not know happened.

All of these excerpts are a peek into such full, lush worlds just the way the best excerpts are. Hope you enjoy them all.

—Hardy Griffin

Bitter Orange Rum

Ony Ratsifandrihamanana

Chapter One

Kamala Rayleigh's pregnancy started in 1970.

It was a blessed year, 1970, a year like you rarely saw in Sambay. In January, hordes of sun-glassed and sun-screened tourists swarmed the seaside promenades lined with bougainvillea trees, and there were so many of them the Governor's office had to decree a new region-wide tax on souvenir shops and seashell jewelry. In March, the Mayor inaugurated the newly-built train station in the midst of the city center, and the fair aristocracy of Sambay stood in line under the scorching sun, with their parasols and feathered hats, for a chance to climb aboard the white *micheline* coach. The first passenger train arrived two days later, transporting the Governor's wife and a year's worth of sugar and rice for the small folk of Sambay, the rickshaw pullers and the vanilla sorters, who squinted suspiciously at the cargo from behind the gates.

In July, the Poet arrived in Sambay by that very same train. He lodged on the first floor of a nameless hostel across from the station; from its window, beyond the tattered acrylic curtains one could see the browning river, and the shantytowns' sparkling metal roofs on the other shore. For two weeks no one knew of his presence. He frequented roadside coffee stalls and queasy, hole-in-the-wall diners in the markets, where both patrons and sellers had never heard of him. When word of his presence finally reached the

Bougainvillea, the whole aristocracy of Sambay rose as one and soon enough the Poet drowned in dinner invitations and marriage proposals. He left before the season's end, unmarried still, with a notebook of poems wet with sea and saltwater.

In August, vanilla beans grew overnight on their stems, and all over the mountains farmers and traffickers toasted to the best harvest of the decade. In September, the President himself came to Sambay, and the legends say he shook so many hands on the way to his hotel that he had to ice them for a whole night to alleviate the cramps. The city elders welcomed him under the customary red canopy, atop the city council steps, and the most wrinkled and venerable of them gawked at him, having fully expected one of those blue-eyed and straight-nosed foreigners from the days of the colony. It was the first time the central power strayed anywhere north of Port-Bergé.

In October, after years of infertility, Kamala Rayleigh announced she was pregnant with what the ultrasounds and the shanty seers promised to be a boy.

Believe it or not, out of all the miraculous things registered that year, Kamala's pregnancy fuelled the most gossip among the flowery patios and sunbathed terraces of the Bougainvillea. Would-be mothers from all over the Sava travelled to Sambay and swarmed the Rayleigh house's marble portico in the hope that Kamala's blessing would ricochet onto them. Priests urged Kamala to give due praise to the Lord in the form of a substantial financial donation to the *Sainte-Thérèse* Chapel of Sambay, while the housemaids wondered which sorcerer she consulted, what potion he prescribed and whether said potions tended to cause varicose veins.

To put the miracle in context: in 1970, Kamala was forty-three years old, and in the *Sainte-Thérèse* Chapel a row of five yellow candles always burned in remembrance of the five children she lost before she even knew she carried them. She was the third out of seven sisters, all prettier and wittier than her. For a long time, everyone thought she would never marry because of the large nervy childhood scar that bloomed on the side of her face. Her marriage with Charles, heir and vice-president to the railroad company, sparked wild rumors of sorcery and love potions, and when she kept miscarrying people sneered that it was divine punishment for her deception. So were things in Sambay, where there was nothing but gossip to fill a stifling summer afternoon. Maybe like Kamala you disapprove of such a pastime. Maybe you too despise small towns. Yet the best stories often come from small towns, for no other reason than there is little else there to do but make up stories.

Stories came plentiful. Kamala was, one must say, an unconventional mother-to-be. In the first days of October, as she strode through the halls of the Franciscan Sisters' Clinic in Sambay, Kamala had expected it to be menopause rather than motherhood ringing the doorbell on her biology. When Doctor Bernardin showed her the fetus on the dark screen, she was simultaneously overcome with a burst of joy and a stab of terror. She barely ate the following evening and went to bed earlier than usual, to her husband's quiet dismay and her mother-in-law's less quiet contempt.

Inside her room, Kamala slipped into bed fully dressed and lay stiff and silent, staring at the avocado tree outside her window and its shadows quivering against the walls.

She thought of the magpie's nest inside the tree, of the candles she lighted every Saturday and of the nieces and nephews she spoiled with gifts and attention, through whom she had resigned after so many rosaries to live motherhood vicariously. She thought of Charles, of the railroad, of her own mother still rotting somewhere in a retirement home. She thought of names and baby shoes, and then as she thought of all of this she fell asleep. When she woke up, Kamala was a different woman.

She appeared at breakfast in a bright pink bathrobe and slippers, and announced that she was pregnant, that it was a miracle from God, and that starting from this instant everything would be done to ensure she delivered the child. Before anyone could react, Kamala decreed, then and there at the breakfast table, a set of a hundred and eighty rules by which anyone wishing to remain under their roof must abide.

Rule number one: no more Saturday night parties, no more jazzy sleepless nights, no more half naked girls wandering the halls in the early mornings, no more khat and no more anti-depressants left on sink rims.

Rule number two: cigarettes, and any substitute (hand-rolled cigars, nicotine pellets, scented hookahs) were henceforth banned from the premises.

Rule number three: all detergents, dishwashing liquids and other household products were to be thrown away and replaced with a concoction of Marseille soap or a mixture of vinegar and baking soda.

Rule number four: no more interior perfumes, no more ylang-ylang deodorants sprayed on the living room pillows, and so on and so forth, the whole morning, as Kamala spouted rule after rule without blinking or pausing to catch her breath, erect with a gleaming determination that her in-laws had never encountered before.

Some of Kamala's rules were sensible, motivated by a trendy desire to switch up the manmade with the natural. Others were obscure and inscrutable, like rule number thirty-three which forbade monkfish soup on Wednesdays.

Kamala forbade salt, locked the brandy in the safe, enforced worship sessions at five in the morning and five in the afternoon. "This house will be a sanctuary, dedicated to health and temperance," she told her stunned in-laws. "Key words will be prayer and serenity. We will no more discuss Nietzsche or Kissinger, but rather Mary Mother of God and her son Jesus Christ the Merciful."

"This is ridiculous," said Kamala's mother-in-law. "Do you want to turn my house into a monastery?"

Kamala pinned her with a blank stare. "This is my house now," she said.

She spent the rest of the day in bed, breathing in and breathing out, listening to seagulls in the bay and the blooming flowers in the garden. When came lunch time, after some hesitation, the maids served broiled leek instead of the monkfish soup that Charles' father so liked. And even though disapprobation hung heavy around the table, Kamala's in-laws complied with her demands.

*

In the opinion of all concerned, including Kamala herself in retrospect, it was a ridiculous time. Every day Kamala went to the Clinic and had Doctor Bernardin examine her. Every two days she visited the Chapel Sainte-Thérèse and had Father Soulemana bless her. Ultrasounds occurred once a week and every two weeks white-clad deacons from the Lutheran Church roared biblical verses in every corner of the Rayleigh house while Kamala followed behind them, clutching a rosary. She could not sleep at night, far too engrossed in all the dangers remaining to be abated, every sin still needing atonement.

Around her third month of pregnancy, Kamala thought

her morning sickness was laced with blood. Convinced this was the work of a malicious hand, she fired the house staff, at the indignation of her sisters-in-law who had grown up cradled and pampered by this indolent domesticity. In replacement, Kamala hired a French dietician from the capital, who was rumored to have worked within the high society of Hollywood in America. For two months he stuffed the family with pumpkin seeds, kale and insect powders, until Charles, asserting his prerogatives as husband and father of the future child, sent him back to the capital on the first Tuesday train.

To canalize her anxiety, Doctor Bernardin advised Kamala to keep a journal. Ever diligent, she bought an account book inside which she tracked every minute change and evolution in her pregnancy, from the color of her stools to the amount of hair she shed after her bath. She also got a calendar. Every morning she ticked a square with a red marker, like a child counting down the days until Christmas. And as she checked the days and noted her every humor, her body swelled, her veins fattened and the skin on her stomach stretched, and inside the watery mystery of her matrix, the Prophet Kuno observed his own conception.

Like his mother, even in the womb Kuno Rayleigh was an unconventional baby. For one, he looked particularly bulky: at four months pregnant, Kamala could barely stand on her legs. Visitors thought she was having twins or triplets but no, there was but a single baby under that dome of quivering flesh. He inspired in her all sorts of bizarre and irrepressible cravings. He woke her at night, yearning for a can of petrol to smell, guava leaves to chew or dirt to eat. In turn Kamala woke the gamekeeper, who cycled all the way to the city center and woke the gas station attendant, the druggist, the pharmacist or any appropriate person—all cited here in the singular, for at the time Sambay was a prototype municipality that only counted one each of what the mayor deemed essential for a modern, prosperous city.

Some days Kamala's cravings transcended the physiological, and she found herself needing to listen to Bach—whom she never liked—or read Balzac—whom she found dull and tedious—or contemplate a Modigliani—whom she deemed blasphemous. "This baby is relentless, and he likes nothing I like," she said to the maids while they fanned her and massaged her wrists. Once, during an ultrasound, Doctor Bernardin heard rumbling waves in his stethoscope instead of the familiar, solid beat of a forming heart. "My son is a poet," Kamala said with a dreamy smile.

Kamala seldom worried about her son's intrauterine quirks. Only the outside world, with its sharp angles and toxic fumes, obsessed her. She was so busy weighing every milligram of salt in her meals and anticipating every possible disease or accident, and everyone else was so busy trying to keep up with her, that no one noticed the weeks trickling by. One morning as she went to check the day on her calendar, Kamala realized that it was November 1971, that the country had changed president and constitution, that it had been six months since the Poet published his last collection, that the train was no more a novelty even in Sambay, that her due date had come and gone without anyone remembering it and that she had now been pregnant for over a year.

*

Once upon a time in the fair town of Sambay, Kuno Rayleigh was not born. In his mother's womb, he slept curled up on himself, tuning out the world outside his amniotic sac and weaving all kinds of strange and incongruous thoughts in the folds of his brain, fully formed yet in no hurry to take his place in the world. Among the strange and incongruous things his mind entertained, Kuno was in particular thinking of his birthplace and the geographical determinism that would govern his life.

In other circumstances—in other places—Kamala Rayleigh, upon noticing her extended pregnancy, would have gone to a hospital full of reputable doctors graduated from major foreign universities, and they would have told her that where women counted their pregnancy in months, doctors spoke of weeks of amenorrhea. The average pregnancy lasted thirty-seven to forty-seven weeks. Over forty-two weeks, the term was considered "exceeded." From forty-three weeks over, the risk of perinatal mortality climbed to five per thousand compared to zero point seven per thousand at thirty-seven weeks. At fifty weeks, Kamala would have been referred to a specialist, who would have informed her that a woman in the province of Yunnan, China, had stayed pregnant for seventeen weeks after term before her doctors allowed her a caesarian, and that another in America was as far as fifty-four weeks when her doctor triggered the labor with the use of a hormone called oxytocin.

However, Kamala was neither in China nor in America, and there was no brilliant and passionate expert in the Franciscan Sisters' Clinic who would have devoted hours leafing through his medical abstracts to figure out the exact medical and hormonal combination that would have helped her give birth as quickly and with as little risk as possible. She was in Sambay, a sleepy little town in the far north of an island in the Indian Ocean, where doctors at the Dispensary and the Clinic—the first for the poor, the latter for the rich—were part-time grocers, where women who wanted a child offered honey on the forest altars, and where a child unborn after a year could only be the work of forces far more mysterious than science.

So instead of going to the hospital, like her husband urged her, or the confessional, like she herself would have wanted, Kamala did what the circumstances entailed and asked for a sorcerer. As if the request was too farfetched for him to process, Charles only asked: "Which one?" Kamala said: "The best."

Seeking the services of the Sava's finest magician was a daunting task for a number of reasons. First, the year was 1971 and in early May the Parliament approved the Witchcraft Suppression Act, Article One of which promised jail, fines, expropriation, excommunication, scorn and malediction for over ten generations to anyone engaging directly or indirectly with any practice of magic or charlatanism. To this concern, Kamala, while drafting an ad for the Sambay Gazette, retorted: "No one cares about the law" which was a succinct but accurate analysis of legal implementation in our country. Second, though theirs was a strictly esthetic form of Catholicism, the Rayleighs were nonetheless one of the founding families of the *Sainte Chapelle de Sambay*. What would it look like turning to sorcery when good Catholic morals would have them rely on God? To this, Kamala licked the rim of the envelope containing the ad for the Sambay Gazette, and said: "The Lord is merciful. He will understand."

Third, the Sava's best wizard was a highly contested title. The North swarmed with prophets and lunatics of all kinds, and everyone had their own opinion on who deserved the distinction. If you asked Isabelle, the Mayor's second wife, for example, she would tell you the best wizard in the

North lived in a little white cottage at the outskirts of Port-Bergé. Doctor Bernardin, however, claimed that the prophet of Port-Bergé was nothing but a conman, and that the real best wizard of the Sava was a blind young man in a fisher's village. Philomène, the new kitchen girl, swore the best wizard around was none other than her uncle Gérard, who once resurrected a little girl using herbal fumigations.

"We'll just meet them all," Kamala decided a week after the Gazette published her ad, when friends, colleagues, servants, neighbors, acquaintances, and even complete strangers accosted them with over fifty candidates. She set the living room with two armchairs and a coffee table, and ordered tea and ginger biscuits. There she sat in regal hugeness, her ankles swollen and puffing out of her loafers, her armpits sweaty and folding over the fabric of her sari.

"I prepared questions, you take notes," she told Charles, who had been observing her in mute and cautious perplexity.

He was reserved, Charles. A childhood immersed in locomotive machinery and rail engineering left him a taste for cogs and traction. As an adult he cultivated austere tendencies, preferring the iron tang of work over worldly vanities. Devoted to his father's company like a monk to God, he maintained a strict celibacy for the longest time, rejecting proposals from all over the region and burying himself in maps and stations plans. When his father threatened to leave the company to one of his cousins should he fail to produce a suitable heir, Charles relented and married Kamala.

They barely knew each other. Like him, Kamala came from a wealthy family. Like him, she was long past the marrying age. They met through one of those social dinners. He was tall and levelheaded, wearing the black-rimmed glasses that made him look like a young politician. He hardly smiled and only ever spoke of wheel-rail interfaces and vanilla prices, yet his intensity caught the listener's attention and only released it when he was done talking. And Kamala, though neither the youngest nor fairest at the table, shone through her dry, educated comments and the disarming honesty of her scarred face. Among the ladies, she was this refined, carnal and Moorish woman, marked by the indolence of people born a bit too late, or too soon.

Seated in front of each other—by destiny or social intervention—they talked about the books they could not find in Sambay's only library, about the time it took to deliver something from the capital, about the railway and the apathy of life in these lands of misty forests and sleepy villages. As they talked, they realized two truths at the exact same time. One, they would never find another soul in the North with whom they connected so well. Second, there would never be more between them than a steady, tender friendship.

"Philomène says some of these sorcerers work for the Devil himself," said Kamala while anxiously fiddling with her rosary. "She says they tell you whatever you want to hear and have you do things you would otherwise never consent to."

Charles, who no more knew how to be a husband than Kamala knew how to be a wife, took a seat next to her. "Then they're no different from the railway's collaborators," he said, and for the next three weeks he stayed with her, pinning charlatan after charlatan with the young businessman's exasperated gaze.

The first candidate came in a navy jacket and a cap with the logo of a foreign football team. His mother wore a prim pink suit and a feathered hat. "Sorry to bother you this early in the morning," she said. "We had a very long trip from Port-Bergé and we have to be back before tomorrow. The Ancient

One has a French exam."

The Ancient One was ten years old. He carried a schoolbag decorated with cartoon stickers and played with a plastic figurine—*Amon the Destroyer*, said his mother, *boys love it, prepare to see him everywhere if yours is a boy.* Before Charles or Kamala could voice their doubts, the Ancient One spoke for the first time. "It's a boy," he said.

Kamala leaned toward him. "Why won't he come out?"

"He doesn't want to."

"What should I do?"

"You don't want him be born either. Glorious boys are calamities for their mothers."

The mother nodded gravely. The Ancient One, his mother, and Amon the Destroyer left an hour later, with the money-filled envelope promised to everyone answering the Sambay Gazette's ad.

"That's a fine pair of hoaxers for sure," said Charles. Kamala stayed thoughtful.

The second candidate came the following day and asked for a pitcher of sugared water. He was dying of thirst, having walked all the way from the extreme north of the country.

"That's two hundred kilometers," said Charles.

"Two hundred and forty-three, to be precise," said the sorcerer.

He had thin shaggy hair and skin as dark and smooth as cut ebony. He wore a filthy woolen cape, beaded necklaces and a tattered loincloth. "The great prince Ibonia was also born late," he said once his thirst had been quenched. "He stayed in his mother's womb for ten years, and had the time to choose a name and a wife, before he came to the world on the steep cliffs of his father's kingdom."

He recommended oleander root tea, which gave Kamala explosive diarrhea but delivered no baby. "This was a bad idea," Charles sighed while dampening her forehead with cold water. Inside his mother's womb, Kuno Rayleigh sympathized.

As the days went on they met different variants of the above two characters. Some descended from sooty huts in the mountains; others drove up from luxurious seaside villas. Some sat on wheelchairs and claimed they met Queen Soazara two centuries ago; others watched the time because they had to go back to school. Some grew up with missionaries and only spoke French or English, and one time, Norwegian. Others mumbled an indigenous and bastardized Arabic that an interpreter translated with great difficulty. Some worked in imports and dabbled in politics. Others lived off donations with the frugality of ascetic monks. Yet all, coming in pilgrimage from all over the Sava, were unanimous: Kamala was blessed and so was her child.

"But why won't he come out?" Kamala asked them, desperate.

"Your son is stubborn," they said. "He will be born when he wants and not a second before."

Kamala ran out of the room and to her chambers, hauling her huge belly, which went on growing like a pumpkin left in its patch. The befuddled doctors at the Clinic assured her everything looked fine, that her baby was due any minute. One day, after yet another ultrasound, Kamala burst into tears in Doctor Bernardin's office and cried so hard and for so long he worried she was going to die there, on the examination table. But eventually she stopped. She asked for a handkerchief, then for the telephone.

Moments later, a shrill ring woke up the dogs in a single-story villa surrounded by coconut trees. After seven and a half rings, the best wizard of the Sava (but that, no one knew) picked up the phone.

*

It always rained when Anil Rayleigh returned to Sambay. Maybe it was because he disliked his hometown: the boulevards where beggars slept at night, the casinos where tourists took family pictures; the cracked asphalt, the tattered rickshaws, the women sorting vanilla pods under the jackfruit trees and the Bougainvillea in their stifling corsets of propriety... Or maybe it was his hometown that disliked him.

Yet as a young man he had been the prince of this city. On the billboards around the roundabouts, it was still him, as a baby, smiling and angelic for a baby diapers ad. In his old high school's honor gallery, it was still his name engraved on the most prestigious cups and medals. It was still his striking face and his silken hair in the heart of many respectable married women—and men—that elicited the most delectable sighs of melancholia. And when a crisis arose, he was still the one to whom his sisters turned for comfort and support.

He took the Thursday morning train to Sambay, and waited for all the other passengers to exit and for the controller to uneasily tell him it was the terminus before he got off. An old butler greeted him on the platform, took his suitcase and led him to the car, inside which Kamala waited. When she saw him she jumped out of her seat and into his arms, and even in her state he could lift her and swing her as if they were still an unruly high school senior and a shy little girl.

"Look at you," Anil cried. "You're huge!"

"You idiot," Kamala said with a smile.

She could not recall the last time she saw him. It could have been two years ago, after they all agreed to commit their mother to a retirement home in the central highlands. Or it could have been at his son's first communion, four years earlier. She wrote him letters and sent birthday cards, and sometimes he would write her back, but he was fickle, busy, and always engrossed in the secrecy of his independent life. He avoided family functions. Sometimes, it seemed he avoided family altogether.

"How are the boys?" Kamala asked when they were in the car.

"Ah, forget about them," Anil said. "It's your boy we need to talk about, right?"

And talk they did, all through the drive to the Rayleigh house, then as they transitioned in the sunny terrace where they were served with bissap tea and warm jalebis, then as they lounged in the rattan chairs and listened to crickets and dragonflies buzz about the rose bushes. The more they talked, the more they relaxed, shedding distance and adulthood. Before long they fell back into the past, into their younger selves who were each other's best friends despite the twelve years difference in age. Back then, Anil was the beloved one, their mother's sweetheart and father's pride. Kamala was the disfigured and tragic little sister. After her accident, her father hired tutors to homeschool her. She spent her days locked behind closed blinds, tearing off the wallpaper and tyrannizing servants, resenting any pity adults would offer her. And still, every day after school Anil would visit her and pull her out of her pit with just his shining smile.

That was how Kamala felt once she stopped talking. As if Anil had shone a light inside the hole she was sitting in, and suddenly all her wallowing and worrying seemed distant and meaningless.

"If you asked me," Anil said after a beat of silence, "I

would say he's waiting for something, your brat."

Kamala sighed. "I don't know what to do anymore."

"You could wait with him. I know, I know. Patience has never been your virtue. But if all those witches are not lying to you—and believe this unrepentant liar, it is very rare that a bunch of liars tell you all the same thing—then I'm just thinking if your kid is still waiting after everything you've already done, he must have a very good reason."

Anil stayed four days, which he spent seducing the house staff, brightening up dinner with anecdotes and emptying the wine cellar. He never stayed more than a week. After a visit he always left everyone breathless, exhausted and elated. The day he left, Kamala followed him to the station. Already anxiety was rising back into her bones, and she wondered when she would hear from him next. In an uncharacteristic show of intimacy, Anil touched the back of his hand to her swollen stomach.

"I dreamed of him," he said.

"The baby?"

"Your son," Anil said, and Kamala wondered whether there was a difference.

"What happened in your dream?" she asked.

"Lots of stuff. School, tennis, marriage... You know, life."

"That sounds to me like a boring dream."

"He will be a real treat. He will love you more than you imagine and give you many sleepless nights. If I were you, I wouldn't worry. I would take this time as a respite because when he gets here, it will all be about him."

The train screeched and smoke fell over the platform. Anil landed a quick peck on Kamala's scarred cheek and jumped on the coach as the train started to move. Kamala stayed until the train disappeared, in the hopes that he would pop out of a window and wave at her, but he never did.

At home, she called Charles.

"What is it?" he asked. "Are you alright?"

"I need a nurse. And medical equipment. And new books."

"What? Why? Are you giving birth?"

"I'm not. But if your son wants to wait, well I will wait for him in the best possible environment. Tell them to bring me a duvet and a hot water bottle, my feet hurt. And tiger balm, I'm sore."

That evening, Kamala settled into her equipped room. There was a medical bed, IV stands and even a wheelchair. In December, when the temperatures soared and the humidity thickened into heavy monsoon rains, the Sambay Gazette published a Saturday column about Kamala, with a grainy picture of her sitting by the window and looking forlorn. Throughout town, salons and kitchens were all about her. Children threw stones at the house and yelled "witch!" until the guard threatened to call their parents. Kamala listened to her sister-in-laws' reports of the outside world and said nothing when they suggested she return to the Clinic. She was determined to wait, must she wait ten years like Prince Ibonia's mother.

*

She did not wait that long. In October of the next year, Irène Ramiadana arrived on the ten a.m. Monday train.

The Hoard:
A Novel of Disordered Family

Sean Gill

Introduction

Muriel Woodworth is under siege. A lifelong hoarder, she has pushed her family away and spends her lonely days at the edge of a dried lake, obsessively playing an addictive mobile game, walled in by tangible reminders of a happier life. In the dead of night, she finds herself the victim of a violent intervention. There are mysteries hidden within Muriel's hoard, and each object has a tale to tell. Sifting through the mess, piece by piece, we learn the winding, dark history of the Woodworth family tree: Luther, Muriel's first husband, an inscrutable long-haul trucker consumed by wanderlust. Her second husband, Rex, a warm-hearted and easily overwhelmed bouncer. Her three mercurial children: Olly, the golden girl and honor student. Jules, the juvenile delinquent. Mal, the invisible son. Each Woodworth bears unique wounds inflicted by the hoard, and they'll fight to make sure they're not buried by it.

SECTION FIVE: 8:52 P.M.

The padlocks swivel, the door chain fastens, and the cylinders slide into place. The unwelcome shadows outside will not darken this threshold. Muriel passes through the garage and tunnels deeper into the house, her movements masked by darkness. On all sides, there are newspapers and plastic storage tubs, old clothing and pill bottles, poster rolls and steamer trunks. No outsider could possibly attribute a sense of order, but to Muriel it is meticulously curated and she knows it as well as the contours of her own mind. Every so often she has to really hunt for something she needs, but isn't that true of memory itself? When you rack your brains for some name or distant piece of information from the internal library?

Each arrangement here is rife with meaning, and even the layers of dust speak to her—they tell the story of the last time she entwined her self with an object. Even more importantly, the dust functions as a security system, letting her know if someone has violated her space without permission (such permission has not been given in many years, and, even then, only to Mal. Oh, and to Olly, too... before she turned unreliable).

You can no longer watch television from the living room sofa. The line of sight to the TV screen is blocked by an escalation of magazines, shoeboxes, clothes, and craft projects which have sort of organically flourished in a bridge-like shape, joining the center table to the couch.

There was a time when you could crawl under the bridge and make it to the VHS cabinet, but since, the space beneath has been filled with supermarket circulars, board games, medical equipment, and stuffed animals. The reason I'm telling you this is because Muriel keeps the shotgun and its ammunition in the VHS cabinet—behind the tapes, for secrecy's sake—and right now she is looking at these obstacles in her path and she's paralyzed. She desperately needs the weapon to make a statement, to scare off the Cleansers, but it's equally important to maintain the order that is carefully braided throughout this room.

The alarm on her phone begins to chirp. It is a welcome distraction to load *VampireQuest*, collect the coin, and gather another drop of holy water for her flask. If the game is truly ending like they say it is, this could be the last holy water she will ever collect. It's painful to think about, but also nice to know it's there.

A knock at the front door. She almost leaps out of her skin. Even though that door couldn't possibly be opened, even with the aid of a battering ram, nobody should ever be on her porch. Even the mailman's daily visit makes her uncomfortable.

"Hey, are you in there?" says a man's voice. From his shadow, she can see that he is shifting his weight from one leg to another. (There's a small window on the door, veiled by a curtain.) "All we want to do is help you."

"You've picked a bad time," she mutters, not quite loud enough to be heard. "The worst time, it's really a bad time, I can't believe this."

She lifts her thigh and tries to step across the bridge. It isn't meant to be. Her foot catches on a shredder box filled with receipts and she falls into the debris, landing on her ribs. She crunches an overloaded plastic laundry basket. Newspapers cushion the blow, but she is sinking as if in quicksand, among dusty towels and a deflated air mattress. Plastic laundry baskets always crack when you overload them; it's the lattice. They're not meant as long-term storage containers. Muriel knows this, but she can't help it. "Oh nooo, no-no-no," she says.

She finds her footing, wriggling beyond the damage she's inflicted, and finds herself facing the VHS cabinet. Reaching over and inside, she feels the butt of the Remington and carefully excavates it, trying not to dislodge *Three Men and a Baby*, *Winchester '73*, *Overboard*, or the double cassette of *Titanic*. With the shotgun in her hands for the first time in nearly a decade, she feels reassured, as if Rex—the old, reliable Rex—is physically present, guiding her movements. Maybe she can scare off the Cleansers so quickly that the Rage Wraith will still be hovering in the backyard afterward, ripe for the taking. But when she reaches for the box of birdshot, there's a second, more urgent, Gestapo-style pounding at the door. Panicking, her hand inadvertently dislodges an entire row of videotapes.

She scrutinizes the welter of tapes landing at her feet with an intense sadness, as each summons an entire host of feelings and associations. *Jerry Maguire*, taped off of television during the night Mal told her about his class field trip to the fish hatchery. *Grease*, a high school graduation gift for Olly, and one she neglected to bring with her to college. *Summer of '42*, which they all watched the afternoon Jules pricked her foot with a rusty nail and needed a tetanus shot. There's one tape among them that she's sure she's never seen before, and as she removes the box of cartridges she sees that it's called

The Story of *The Dinosaur Murders*

VHS Tape in box with promotional insert.

Cardboard, plastic, Philips head screws, magnetic ribbon, glossy insert promising a mail-in offer: "3 films for 99¢, your choice, including Brainscan, In the Mouth of Madness, *and* Needful Things.*"*
7 3/8 x 4 1/16 x 1 inches.

Ooh, this is a good one, though I have to admit it's a bit

of an acquired taste. *The Dinosaur Murders* ain't for everybody. It's like Bobcat Goldthwait, watching golf, or dipping your french fries in your milkshake—you're either gonna love it or you're gonna hate it.

First, a little background: when Muriel told Rex that she wanted him to get to know her kids, he assumed she'd at least be present for the gathering. Instead, Muriel is off on some urgent and nebulous errand while he's about to host Olly, Jules, and Mal at his place for an entire evening. He's given some advance notice of the situation and, knowing it is Mal's birthday week (he's turning eleven), he stops by the video store beforehand and browses the "previously rented" section, where used tapes are available for four dollars apiece. He's heard the kid has seen *Jurassic Park* about three hundred times so he figures *The Dinosaur Murders* will be right up his alley.

Rex faces a quandary. Even though it's Mal's birthday, to shower attention only on the boy would risk alienating the girls the very first time he meets them. He doesn't know what an appropriate present for a teenage girl is, but he's already at the video store and trying not to overthink it. He knows Olly is going to college, so he grabs a copy of *Sommersby* for her (it looks like some sappy, high-brow romantic shit with Richard Gere, Jodie Foster, and historical costumes). He knows Jules is "difficult" and has been having trouble at school, so he buys her a copy of *Problem Child 2*. This is mostly because he was pressed for time and couldn't think of a better idea, but he also figures it could be a subtle, funny way for the two of them to communicate, to wink and nod at the elephant in the room.

He rehearses a few different speeches, but when the kids arrive on his doorstep he launches straight into this one: "Y'all can call me Rex. Your mom and I have been seeing each other for about six weeks, I know you've been told. I'm not a stranger to loss, and I'm not gonna give you any pretty words or try to replace your dad and that's not what this is about. It's about how I'd like to get to know you because your mom means a lot to me. Now come on inside." Only after he's finished the monologue does he take a moment to breathe and register the children's presence.

"Thank you, Mr. Everhardt," says Olly. She has straight brown hair, a high forehead, widely spaced eyes, and a painfully shy demeanor. While her teeth are straight (the braces came off months ago), her smile is aslant, unsure of itself.

"Okay," says Jules. She has hunched shoulders and a perpetual scowl. Her haircut's a lopsided, center-parted bowl that hangs low over her face, fully obscuring one of her eyes. She's wearing a rumpled plaid button-up clearly intended for a grown man.

"This place is cool," says Mal. He's a skinny, wide-eyed kid in a Garfield T-shirt who is somehow sporting dual cowlicks despite having such closely cropped hair. In fact, the haircut looks like it may have been self-inflicted.

Rex's apartment *is* cool. It's clean for a bachelor pad, relatively spacious, and possessing many metropolitan-style fixtures the children have only seen on TV: a cast iron radiator, a futon, an industrial spool table, a bean bag chair, a peephole on the door. They step inside, and though Rex attempts to herd them toward the futon, they stand awkwardly beyond the threshold, Olly clutching her textbooks, Jules looking out the window, and Mal perusing the cinder block shelf below a Guns N' Roses poster.

"Do you have any books about dinosaurs?" Mal asks.

"Let's see," says Rex. "You can probably tell a lot about a man from the things he has on his bookshelf." (There are no books on dinosaurs, though there are a few on baseball, drag racing, the U.S. Marine Corps, and *Saturday Night Live*. If they perused his bathroom, they'd find *Uncle John's Bathroom Reader* and a *Playboy*-branded book of party jokes.)

Jules kneels down and tugs on a coffee-table-book-sized volume with spiral binding. On its metallic cover, it says "SEX."

"This book says 'sex' on it," says Jules.

"That's not for children," says Rex, sliding it back onto the shelf. "It's Madonna's book, a friend got it for me as a gag."

"A lady friend?" says Jules. Recently, with strangers, she's been saying aloud the first sarcastic thing that pops into her head, and she's finding that this comes with a certain amount of power.

Blushing, Rex says, "Have a seat on the futon. Can I get y'all sodas? I have Slice, Jolt, and, uh, grape."

"I'll just have a glass of water, thank you," answers Olly. "Grape for me, please," says Mal.

Jules rolls her eyes. "Could never say 'no' to a Jolt." She follows him into the kitchen, and, as he's wrestling ice cubes out of a stubborn tray, she says, "Ever wonder why she hasn't had you over yet?"

"What?"

"To our house." Jules is as enthusiastic as she's been all week, maybe all year. She's practically glowing. Tucking her hair behind her ear (so she can witness Rex's reaction with both eyes), she says, "You don't think it's weird that she only comes over here? That she sends her kids to meet you at *your* place?"

"I don't know."

"Red alert, Rexy. She's got maj problems."

He smirks, playing it off. "I don't know what you want me to say." "You haven't wondered about it? Not at all?"

"She said she was a packrat. She has a clutter problem and is a little embarrassed. I get that."

"You *don't* get it, Rex. The house is a disaster area. Straight up. Nobody goes in, nobody goes out. Except for us."

Rex laughs. "I know that's not true."

Jules shrugs her shoulders. Her arched eyebrows seem to say, *believe me if you want, I don't care.*

An excruciating moment passes. Rex pops the top on a soda. Maybe he twitches. "I'm gonna run away as soon as I have the chance," she says.

"No, you're not," Rex says, but it's a blind reaction. His mind is elsewhere: he can't stop thinking about an excursion he made earlier in the day, before the video store. He was at a Zales inside the Sweetwater Acres Mall, browsing the engagement rings. Not to propose—not yet—just to sorta look, you know? Conjuring a vision of Muriel, statuesque and resilient, he doesn't quite see how Jules, so cynical and derisive, could be her mother's daughter.

"You'll run away, too. And you can come talk to me about it when you're ready. I'm an expert. I've been planning since I was six. I need to do it. It's the only thing I need. Have you ever needed anything, Rex? Needed it so bad you thought about it every second?"

"This is ridiculous," says Rex, and he offers a shy and awkward smile. He can't let her see it, but the kid is shaking him to the core. He needs to have Muriel here, to refute this nonsense.

Clearly there's a grain of truth to what she's saying, but Jules is trouble, everybody says so. "I'm serious. When you were my age, what did you *need?*"

He exhales. "I 'needed' to be a professional baseball player. And that was silly. I was so sure I needed it, and, you know what? I didn't. Hey, I know what it's like to think you know everything. But you don't. I think if you listened to your mom a little bit more, just *listened*—"

"Oh boy, there's a lot you have to learn. Did she tell you she had a job?"

"No." Rex is pouring the soda. Purple foam blooms between the ice cubes and thousands of tiny bubbles rise to the surface. He's always found the sound reassuring.

"Honesty? That's interesting. We got a big sum of money when Dad died. Life insurance. She'll have to go back to work eventually. But isn't it sort of interesting how *busy* she gets without having a job?"

"She has three kids to take care of. And from what I've heard, not every one of 'em is a Sunday picnic."

Jules sips her soda and laughs. "That's good, Rex. Anyway, I'm gonna have my Jolt, and then I'm gonna leave. I'll be back around eleven."

Rex chews on his lip. "Seems like you got this all figured out." He kicks open the fridge, pulls out a Molson Ice, and, in a bit of masculine performance art, opens it with his BiC lighter. He's relatively sure that any fifteen-year-old should appreciate the display of elder coolness. "Well," he sighs, "I'm gonna head to the living room, have a cold beer, and get to know your siblings."

"Hey, Rex." Jules' eyes have turned hard and challenging. "You really gonna stick around, you know, with Mom?"

When she asks this, he's carrying his beer and two other glasses clustered between his palms in a triangulation of pressure, a technique he learned from the servers at work. He feels taken off-guard and is trying to maintain the balance of the perspiring glasses. "I don't know, that was the plan, I guess. You seem to be trying your best to stop it."

"Will you stand up for Mal? Cause no one was around to stand up for us. Do that, and you'll win my respect. Not love, but respect."

"Sure," says Rex. He wants to ask what that really means, to ask about Luther and what he was like before he died, but curiosity in this time and place would be a form of weakness. He shouldn't be talking about serious matters with a fifteen-year-old, anyway.

In the living room, it's hard for him to be present. He finds himself thinking too much about what Jules said in the kitchen, and he sees her over there, somber, issuing a withering stare. Is she somehow threatening him? There's something emotionally intimidating about the girl, and her sheer presence is only twisting the knife. It's a relief when she excuses herself and walks out the front door. That kid has too much nerve by half.

"Where's Jules going?" asks Olly.

"I gave her permission to go out. She'll be back later. I thought the three of us could watch a movie. I've got microwave popcorn, extra butter."

Failing to find a coaster, Olly gently sets her water glass on the spool. She straightens her spine and clasps her hands together, like a prize pupil in finishing school. "Actually, Mr. Everhardt, if you'll excuse me, too, I have to study. I can set up my books in your kitchen, I won't be a bother to anybody."

"Study?" says Rex. It felt like an adult decision to let Jules go free, but now he's feeling like a captain, mid-mutiny. "From what I heard, you already nailed it, got the free ride and everything. Isn't this when you get to enjoy some senioritis, kick back, and relax?"

"No," says Olly. "I'm taking five AP classes and have seven AP tests scheduled across the next three weeks." (Even though she hasn't taken the classes, she had enough confidence in her private study of Art History and Statistics to sign up for those tests, too.)

"AP what, now?"

"Advanced Placement classes. It's going to make the difference with my college credit. If I score perfect fives, I can start off with twenty-eight credit hours. That's more than two semesters' worth."

This is a lot of information for Rex. "Why would you want to cut your college short? Everybody says it's the best time of your life."

"My life will begin after college." Olly says this with a hint of casual melancholy, as if she has often repeated it to herself like a mantra. (She has.)

"Well, okay... lemme clear off the table." Rex dumps his empty and grabs another Molson. There isn't anything to clear off of the kitchen table except for a bunch of bananas, a hand gripper, and a box of Frosted Flakes. He remembers the videotapes and thinks it's just as well that Jules left; he'd feel weird giving her *Problem Child 2* now that they'd shared such a heavy conversation. Stepping into his bedroom to retrieve the tapes, he sees Muriel's pajamas lying askew on a seat-back. He hopes he's not fucking this up.

Olly is already spread out on the kitchen table, her textbooks and papers scattered everywhere.

"I got this for you," says Rex.

"Oh... uh, thanks," says Olly, taking the cassette. She's looking at the front cover, where Richard Gere holds an oil lamp and Jodie Foster holds his hand.

"Do you own it already?"

"Uh... no." Reading from the back cover, she recites,

"People remember Jack Sommersby. They know him as a bitter, loutish man. But when Jack returns to his hometown after the Civil War, he's tender, caring, and resourceful. Has the war changed him... or is the man calling himself Jack Sommersby an imposter?"

"I haven't seen it. It just looked like a smart movie for a smart young lady."

"Thank you," says Olly, but the tape has already been cast aside and her nose buried in her calculus textbook. Her studies are a tidy little wall she's erected for herself, a bulwark against the Bad Times. There's not a chance she'll let Rex inside.

"Oh for two," Rex mutters to himself, slapping *The Dinosaur Murders* against his thigh with a satisfying rattle. "Let's see if you can strike out, huh, big guy?"

Mal is paging through *A Brief History of Drag Racing* when Rex flops beside him on the futon.

"Hey, buddy, you like cars?"

"They're interesting, but I prefer airplanes and spaceships." says Mal.

"That there is the Green Monster," says Rex. He points at an image of a vehicle that is only a car in the most rudimentary sense; it looks more like a jet engine with wheels. "They set the land speed record in that thing. My dad and brother watched 'em race it, back in the day. I was too young to bring to the speedway."

"That's neat."

Rex senses that Mal is humoring him, so he brings out the big guns. "Take a look at this, kiddo. Movie night: *The Dinosaur Murders*. Happy birthday."

"Wow!" says Mal, with genuine enthusiasm. He admires the cover art, where a fearsome dinosaur, probably a Deinonychus, appears to be slashing its way out of the box.

He gushes at Rex about how most of his prized possessions relate to dinosaurs: there are the cheap, rubbery, non-scientifically accurate figures with shockingly sharp claws and teeth; his mini-library of dinosaur-related books; a collection of dinosaur stamps; Grow Monster foam dinosaurs that expand from tiny, water-soluble capsules; plywood, DIY dinosaur skeletons; a mail-in cereal bowl from Universal Studios; and a video copy of *Jurassic Park*, taped off the television but with the commercials omitted. (He has a preternatural sense for when a commercial will be the last in its block and is always quick with the Record button.)

He has bored almost everyone in his family at some point or another with his paleontological knowledge, and he's blissfully waxing lyrical about the common misconceptions casual viewers have about *Jurassic Park*, like the true, relative size of Velociraptors and Dilophosauri, the fallacious lack of feathers, and the fact that so many of the creatures didn't actually originate from the Jurassic period (perhaps a more accurate title would have been *Cretaceous Park*). Rex is happy to listen because it makes him feel like he's doing something right, and it truly warms his heart when Mal asks if he can call him "T-Rex."

Olly does not protest when Rex pops the popcorn, though the sound (and the smell) clearly interferes with her concentration. As Rex and Mal settle in for the movie, she dons her orange foam headphones and begins playing a tape of the Brandenburg Concertos on her Walkman.

Rex lowers the lights, pops the cassette in the VCR, and unruly static is tamed by a familiar FBI warning. Right off the bat, *The Dinosaur Murders* establishes itself as a decidedly off-brand film, chock full of stock music and heavily (perhaps even litigiously) influenced by *Jurassic Park*'s premise of cloned dinosaurs running wild. High-tech medical labs are bare white rooms in a rented office building, decorated with flashing lights and bubbling beakers dyed with food coloring. Stilted and unbelievable dialogue is delivered by amateur actors who can hardly keep their faces straight. When a dinosaur first appears, it's a Frankenstein's monster of papier-mâché, rubber, and assorted puppet paraphernalia. Soon thereafter, it's biting one of the scientists, who screams noisily as fake blood (so bright it's nearly traffic-cone orange) geysers forth from his neck. His body convulses as arterial spray splatters on drywall.

Rex is cackling at the cheapness of the tableau and just about ready for another beer when he looks over at Mal, whose motionless face is streaked with tears.

"Hey, buddy, you okay?" Mal nods.

Panic strikes Rex, right in the diaphragm. "You want me to turn it off?" Mal is silent.

"Okay, I'm gonna stop it." Rex ejects the tape. His heart is pounding. He noticed the "R"- rating earlier, it's true, but he figured if the kid enjoyed *Jurassic Park* so much, isn't that just a bunch of dinosaurs eating people anyway?

Mal doesn't want to be a baby, but he was momentarily overwhelmed by the pure viscerality of the horror, the blood, and, particularly, the screams. It's making him feel gross inside, strangely ashamed, and wishing he could unsee the images, like when Timmy Bailey showed him his collection of Garbage Pail Kids cards.

Rex is thinking about consequences: how he blew this, how he's managed to fucking scar the kid for life on their first meeting, how Muriel will hate him forever, how Jules specifically asked him to stand up for Mal, and what's the first thing he did? Tore him down.

He knows he must do something to set it right, and must perform some essential and fatherly action, but he doesn't have any time to mull it over. It's so damn quiet and the kid looks so agitated, so Rex puts a ballgame on the TV first, to give them a little background noise.

"You like baseball, Mal?"

"I don't know."

Rex can see the kid is putting a considerable effort into not crying all over again, and that makes him feel even worse. "Did your, uh, dad like baseball?"

"No."

"Do you like baseball?"

"I like kickball, I guess."

"Hey, I know that was scary. I didn't know how scary it was gonna be. *I* was even a little scared, I think."

"I'm sorry, Mr. Everhardt." He knows that Rex was trying to do something nice for him, putting so much thought and care into getting him something for his birthday, and he messed it all up by being a big cry-baby.

"No, no, don't you apologize, I'm the one who's sorry." Rex sits down next to Mal and tries to comfort him by placing a hand on his shoulder, but the kid flinches. Hard. For a second he gapes at Mal, who remains frozen, mid-wince, his neck held at a weird angle. "Did you think I was gonna hit you?"

Mal considers this for an uncomfortable amount of time. "No," he says.

"You shouldn't take that movie seriously. It's really, really dumb. It's just a fun, dumb time, something for people to laugh at, like when somebody slips on a banana peel."

"I know."

"Here," he says, retrieving the cassette and sliding it back inside its sleeve. "Why don't you hang on to this, forget all about it, and take a look at it when you're older. Trust me, you'll see how silly it is, and how it was nothing to be scared of."

Is that good advice? It's probably bad advice—the kid will hang on to it and each time he sees it he'll be scared all over again—but Rex has already given it, and while he doesn't know much about being a dad, there's a general sense that being consistent is more important than being right.

"Okay," says Mal, taking the tape.

"Let's watch the game, huh? I'll get you another grape soda."

"Okay."

In the kitchen, Olly is hunched over the table in a world of her own, headphones blazing.

Jules is in a supermarket parking lot doing whippets with her friends. Mal is on the futon, scrutinizing the dinosaur on the video cover, wondering how to reconcile the pit in his stomach with what used to be his favorite thing in the world. Rex wrests another cube from the tray and finds himself thinking about icebergs. Specifically, their tips.

Nat & Z

Olivia Strauss

Chapter 18: The Rescue Mission

As promised, Mom let me spend the rest of the afternoon looking for Z. She dropped me off in front of Z's house. "Be home for dinner. Early dinner. 5pm. On the dot. See you then," she said. Her car peeled away from the curb with a screech.

I was grateful to be alone. I wanted to be alone, or with Z, back in her room watching a movie, legs twisted up together on her bed, eating ice cream, three or four months ago.

I'd spent the entire car ride phone in hand, hoping to hear from Z and planning out my search and rescue mission. I stayed open and ready for a text, call, email, letter, smoke signal, message in a bottle, skywriting. Looking out the window, I scanned all bushes, trees, and sidewalks for messenger pigeons, street signs with altered directions, and stranded kites with notes scribbled on their tails. Anything to keep out the images of Zombie Z stumbling through worst-case scenarios in my head. My imagination flew across the country and toured the coast picturing Zombie Z drunk on a beach, stranded in the mountains, dead on a boat, on the lam in a plane.

The not-knowing-where-Z-was loomed unbearably big. Losing track of her was like misplacing a part of myself, something important like a thumb or synaptic nerve. The hole left behind was a burning emptiness being gnawed bigger by terror's teeth.

Z was missing. To find her I had to think like a detective and scour every inch of Z's world for clues.

First order of business—breaking into the dark and empty house. Well, no, not exactly breaking in. More like legally and safely entering the house using the secret key Brooke kept hidden under a flowerpot by the garage doors. No cars in sight.

I pitter-pattered up the driveway. A lyric from *Love Traffic Controller*, my favorite Chrissy Lee album, played in my head: *I swallow my tears, drown out my fears, me and you, me and you, time in retrograde, moving too fast.*

I cracked my knuckles the way Z did and eyed the trashcan where I knew *N.P.P.* sat rotting in vomit. I crouched down next to the flowerpot and was about to fish out the key when a skunky smell floated past my nose. I froze.

I knew that smell.

I hated that smell.

I was nostalgic for that smell.

Weed.

I followed the scent around the side of the garage and saw something no one in the world would ever expect to see—

The door to Grammy's Ghost's Resting Place was wide open, the passageway that led to the stairwell up to the abandoned apartment.

The sacred seal had been broken. I couldn't help peeking around the yard for the ghost of 91-year-old Swiss woman.

I felt hollow. Not just empty, but carved out. Like I could blow away. I rested my hands on the doorway. I could barely swallow around the lump growing in my throat.

A cold wind slapped my face and shoved me inside.

*

The rest of the afternoon unfolded in slow-motion—a surreal piece of theater in which I was both actor and audience.

I crept into the apartment above Z's garage. The dim space was hot enough to make my skin itch. My back to the door, I inventoried the room; a graying sheet of plastic curtained the would-be kitchen area, a pile of old tools lay scattered from their rusty red toolbox, a well-worn floral couch, a splintering coffee table, a shiny new bar stool, a stack of soggy cardboard boxes, an uninstalled gas stove, loose nails and screws strewn and stuck in the yellowing oatmeal-colored carpeting, an unlit hallway extending black-hole-like to another room. Dust muted every color. The whole place was sad like some abandoned film set. Objects left in tableau, forgotten intentions, unfilled purposes, all left to wait.

I remembered a rant of Ben's about how all good superhero movies had fight scenes staged in construction sites. Something about how the liminal space was a crossroads between new and old, broken and fixed, fear and hope, past and present, stability and insecurity.

I paused at the bar stool—two glasses of water sat on the seat, a perfectly-formed lipstick stain left behind on one of the rims. *Orgasm Red.*

"Babe, you back?" a voice drifted down from the narrow hall. I swallowed the bile in the back of my throat. My heartbeat fluttered, almost as if departing from my chest. I was a ghost in this ghostly space being summoned by the words of a seance. "Babe? That you?" My feet floated down the hallway, hushed by the dust.

Be cool. Be cool. Just be cool. Be cool. Be cool. Just—

"Hurry up sexy!" the voice called.

A door was open—I froze on the threshold—I looked inside as my mouth fell open.

Slouched on the bed was a naked girl with nipples much bigger and darker than mine. A scarf was draped across her lap like the sash of a goddess in a Renaissance fresco.

The naked girl was squinting at me. I blinked back at her. A moment of mutual non- recognition. It wasn't Z.

Who is that? we thought.

She turned and her long bangs fell from her ear and over her face. Her hands searched for something next to her in the sheets. The bed had no frame, no boxspring—just a mattress on the floor. The girl set aside the ashtray of joints and cigarettes nested between her legs, then rummaged through a backpack atop the cardboard box serving as bedside table. On the other side of the mattress, a second backpack leaned against a bar stool. On the stool: a glasses case, a lighter, a plugged-in radio. Discarded clothes carpeted the floor. I realized I was standing on a pair of blue lacy underwear and a cheetah print bra. But I wasn't prepared to reposition myself just then.

The girl hadn't found what she was digging for and she swept her bangs up from her eyes for a better view. Her armpits were unshaved—the thick black patch reminded me of pubic hair.

"Men are hairy," Mom would've chimed in. "*Men* are hairy."

The naked girl bumped the lampshade and the light shifted, spotlighting the pale skin of her breasts and the fading tan lines of a string-bikini. As she leaned over, her breasts hung, and I watched them jiggle, sway, and almost seem to nod. *Uh-huh, uh-huh, uh-huh.* The girl picked through a pile of shirts but didn't put any of them on. As she straightened up, the padlock pendant of her silver chain necklace came to rest in-between her breasts, right below the dyed-red tips of her brown hair. The lock sparkled, reflecting the light, and what I was seeing began to make sense.

In front of me, Tori sat naked. On a mattress. On a floor. In an apartment. In Z's garage.

I'd never seen her without her glasses, let alone a shirt. Tori was basically blind without her glasses and she squinted at me again.

"By the radio," I said, my throat dry. I pointed a little too theatrically to her glasses.

"God, how do you know that?" she grumbled.

Even with her glasses on, Tori didn't grab a shirt. Didn't cross her arms either. Made no move to cover anything. Instead, she leaned back, her arms out behind her on the mattress, effectively shoving her breasts at me. They looked fuller, rounder, curves of shadow beneath them. Her nipples were firm, erect. I thought of my grandma testing melons at the grocery store.

"Eyes up here, Natalie," Tori said with the sinister tone of a cartoon bully and the toothy grin of a coyote. I gulped.

"What are you even doing here?" she asked. She looked right at me, through me—I gulped again. "Trying to find Z," I said, goosebumps bristling up my thighs.

Tori snorted out a laugh, "Yeah, right. You were spying on us. Like you always do."

Her seance resumed, her words called me closer, I took a ghostly step into the room, body flickering with heat, the bra crumpling underfoot.

"You know she knows, right?" Tori shifted her weight, making a show of examining her nails. Her breasts swung to one side.

I opened my mouth, closed it again, inched forward.

"It's pathetic," she said, "Following us around like a lost puppy. When are you going to admit that she is with me?"

"I'm her best friend," I said.

"I don't need to compete with that." Tori's words sliced the air and stuck in my side like a thousand thorns.

I could only gasp. I hadn't ever talked this long with Tori before. I was treading water and didn't know how long I'd last.

"Sophomores," Tori scoffed to herself, perusing the menu of joints in the ashtray. She picked one, lit it, took a deep hit. Smoke crept up between us. I coughed.

The front door slammed shut. Z's voice rang down the hall: "Babe! I got it! I'm back! Shit, I can't believe I found it!"

Z ran into the bedroom, waving a pad of paper over her head like a winning ticket. "Nat?" The second she saw me the goofy smile on her flushed face dropped. "Shit." The pad of paper flapped to the floor as she fumbled in her jacket pocket for a bottle of eyedrops. She doused her red eyes wishfully.

"What are you doing here? I mean, hi, but…what are you doing here?" Z blinked at me and the bed and back. Tori—*still naked*—rolled another joint.

"Hey babe. I don't know, ask her," Tori said, tilting her head at me. She licked the edge of her rolling paper with the tip of her tongue. A drop of sweat sped down my spine. Only my underwear band stopped it from rolling into my butt. *Thank you underwear.*

"Nat, what's wrong?" Z stepped toward me.

I stepped back.

A dance of betrayal.

"I thought you were dead," I whispered.

"What?" Z said, with a grunted laugh.

"Where have you been?" I asked.

"What does it matter?"

"Your mom thought you were with me."

"Yeah, and?" Z shrugged, grabbing the pad of paper from the floor and slapping the dust off on her leg. It was Dr. Mom's prescription pad from the hospital.

"Why do you have that?" I asked, my heart in my throat.

Z cracked her knuckles and shifted from foot to foot. She even made her toes crack.

"What are you doing with it?" I said.

"Nothing you need to worry about."

"Are you sick?"

Z pushed past me and stuffed the prescription pad into the backpack across the room. "I don't need you judging me!" she said over her shoulder. There was mud on her jacket. I remembered everything I'd seen before: the medication bottles, the pills, the fully stocked drug room. I imagined everything I hadn't seen, too: the other parties, the other pills, the other drug rooms.

"Is *that* what you've been doing with her?" I asked.

Z whirled around on me, eyes squeezing shut before flashing open. "It's none of your business what I do with my girlfriend!"

Z's voice banged around the walls of the empty room and buzzed into silence.

In between us was the mattress, on the mattress was Tori—the apex of our triangle. I hated Tori in that moment, on a structural level, but also on a deeply biological level. The hatred was coded in my DNA at that point. Tori was smoking a joint and reading a damn newspaper. No apology. No excuses. Still here. *Still naked.*

Back when Z and I were both outsiders looking in, we overheard Tori in the senior nook ranting about how she reads the news in order to '*keep an eye on the patriarchy*'— that way she can '*use the system to destroy the system.*' I rolled my eyes then, I rolled my eyes now. I could already feel myself rolling them later, in whatever world would exist after this.

"And in Grammy's apartment—" I said.

"Come on, Nat. Grow up," Z said.

"Disturbing Grammy's ghost."

"That's not real, Nat! None of that was real!"

"Yeah but—"

Z erupted again.

"What I do with my girlfriend and where I do it is none of your goddamn business! Not anymore!" she yelled.

Suddenly I was so tired, heavy in my body. I desperately needed to cry. Or *sob*. I dug my fingernails into my palms, to hold back the overflow of anger and grief and confusion. The lump in my throat scratched and tugged at me, wanting to tear me in two.

With a ragged inhale I said, "It's my business when your mom calls me."

Z's eyebrows shot up. "She called you?"

"Wondering where you are. You weren't answering your phone."

"You could've lied."

"I didn't know where you were," my voice a small draft of air escaping my lungs. "I worried."

"You don't need to know where I am ALL the time, Nat." Her eyes went hollow, voice went cold. I didn't recognize it, except that it sounded like Tori's. Z—the corpse of her former self, possessed, ventriloquized. I felt gut-punched.

"Caring about you," I said, "that's not something that just goes away. Worry isn't something that just turns off—"

Z cut me off with a sigh and crossed her arms. "I refuse to feel bad for having a life!"

I struggled to speak, the words squeezing past the lump in my throat: "I...I have...I've been on the outside for so long...."

"I have a girlfriend, Nat! I want to spend time with her. That's normal, okay? It's a normal thing to do!"

"Yeah, but—" I tried again.

Like a lightbulb turning on, Z came back to life, her possession over, she started shaking her head *no, no, no*, the shine in her eyes warmed her face, and her voice was hers again, familiar.

"I mean, half the time I'm not even good enough to be with her! She's amazing, I wish you saw that. And I'm pissed that you don't. She's so amazing and I'm not good enough. I try so hard, but I'm actually lame, too lame for her. You know how much pressure that is? Everyday, I just pretend that I'm not an idiot. I pretend that I'm who she thinks I am," Z pointed at Tori. Tori turned a page and kept reading the news. "I spiral so bad I have to give myself Nat-style pep talks in my head."

"You've ignored me for months," I said. My furrowing eyebrows were bringing on a headache.

"Ignore you?" Z flung her arms up. "You're literally everywhere! Following me around, spying on me, taking notes. It's weird!"

My eyes watered. "I miss you," I said.

"Shit, Nat. You think it was easy for me to see you climbing our tree or hiding by the nook and *not* say anything? You think it was easy for me to shut you out? I wanted to wave at you! I wanted to wave at you every damn time I saw you spying on us."

"Why didn't you?" I could barely tell if I was whispering or screaming.

"Because we were losers, Nat!" Z was yelling, "We never did anything! We never went to parties, we never hung out with anyone, we never tried anything new! And now I have a chance to really *experience* something," Z's hands wildly punched and pointed through the air, punctuating her words. She paced back and forth, taking her turn crushing the bra underfoot.

"At least we were together!" I said. My body shook—it was a giant bruise being pressed and pressed and pressed.

She stopped pacing and pointed at me.

"You think we could stay that way forever?"

"Why not?" I said.

"I did this for us," Z said. "*We* planned this. *Our* move up the social ladder. *Us* becoming cool. I opened doors for *us*, Nat! But you didn't walk through any! I wanted you to come with me. I tried. I really did. But you did nothing. That's not my fault! I tried to bring you."

"Yeah, but we were best friends."

The room was tiny and way too hot. Suffocating.

"Oh, Nat." Z looked at me with wide eyes. "We were losers."

"You were the coolest person I know."

"Stop, okay? Just stop."

"Stop what?"

"Stop trying to flirt with me. I'm with Tori. You're not my girlfriend. We were never together."

The ache in my chest cracked open and the tears came, hot and gushing, vision gone. "We told each other everything—"

"Things change, Nat! You have to learn that!"

Her words were the final blow of the hammer, the cracks spread and I shattered into a million pieces, scattered across the bedroom. I shut my eyes, went internal, into my sadness and anger, reaching for what was left of me. I wanted my waves of tears to carry me out of my body and into the world. I wanted relief.

Spontaneously, the voice I've always kept inside, the one I speak to myself with, the one that sings in my journal, screams in my poems, the one my mom has never heard, spoke up: "I don't want change! I want what we had! We held hands. We kept each other's secrets. We slept in the same bed. So what were we?" I was on the stand arguing my defense, shaking, guilty.

"Friends, Nat." Z stuffed her hands into her pockets. I balled mine into fists.

"We kissed," I said.

"You're straight," Z said with a shrug.

Straight. The word was a small metal box, no air holes, and I was inside, suffocating. *I'm going to die in this box. Straight.*

The rise of my voice had its fall. It shriveled and buried itself deeper than ever in my chest.

Outside, wind howled through the trees. A dog whined and barked.

In the bedroom, the gravely inhale of my breath, the crack of Z's knuckles, silence.

The obnoxious rustling of a newspaper.

Tori—who had stayed quiet this *entire* conversation—took her time folding the newspaper, stubbed out her joint, stretched a leg long, and looked up at me. She pushed her glasses up her nose and smiled crookedly.

Her line sounded rehearsed: "It's not an intimate relationship if you're not fucking."

*

I came back home to find Mom in my bedroom reading my diary.

Chapter 19: The Retreat

All winter break, I hid out at my dad's house.

On our first night together, Dad and I sat in old beach chairs sunken into melting snow, scooted up to the lip of the metal fire pit on the lawn. We built a fire, made s'mores and let the sticky goo of marshmallow and melted chocolate dry on our chins and hands. More than once, a marshmallow of mine erupted into flame, softened, and fell from my stick, feeding the fire.

"Okay kiddo, I'm heading in for the night," Dad said. He stood up and ditched his s'more branch into the fire. "You coming?"

"Not yet," I said.

"The fire will die out on its own when you're done." Dad patted me on the shoulder and went inside.

Starlight poked through the deep darkness of the night. I widened my eyes and inhaled, the air chilling my bottom molars. I felt like a creature of the night—a fiery owl blinking awake with the moon, free to fly.

With Dad gone, I pulled out the spy notebook from my coat pocket. For the last time I read the words scrawled on the inside cover—*Operation Getting to Know Tori James*.

I inserted the notebook into the flames, like dropping an envelope into a mailbox.

I realized I didn't know where Z's coming out letter was anymore. If I did, I would have burned it, too. The letter was somewhere, or nowhere. I probably lost it weeks ago. Maybe it fell out of my pocket while I was spying from the bushes behind school—maybe the letter was there, shivering in the dirt, afraid and alone. Or a branch had skewered it while I climbed my lookout tree for a view of the parking lot. Or I'd forgot to remove the letter from my pants' pocket before doing laundry, and it died a sudsy death, waterlogged into silence then cremated in a dryer.

I looked up at the moon until the moon turned blurry. I trudged inside and slept deeply blanketed in the lingering smell of campfire.

*

I spent the other thirteen days of break detoxing.

Rehabbing?

Retreating?

Crying? Well, only once, at the cutest mouse I'd ever seen, sobbing in the no-kill trap under Dad's kitchen sink.

Mornings, I needed no alarm clock—sounds were enough. Inside: the radiators announced themselves with creaks, clangs, and whistles. Outside: the chatter of birds eating a breakfast of seeds and nuts from the backyard feeder, a chirped symphony.

From the triangle window high above my bed, winter light, soft and warm, spread across my orange polka-a-dot comforter. I stretched, yawning awake. The vaulted ceilings ribbed with dark wood beams, the paneled walls stained a deep cherry, the steel spiral staircase painted white—it all made the loft-style bedroom feel like an upscale pirate ship. I liked pretending that I was the captain, setting sail at night, docking each morning.

I squeezed my eyes shut, trying to focus on the bird musical out back. I wanted to prosecute Z in the grand and cinematic courtroom of my thoughts. A jury of our peers (Lisa, Eve, the entire Powers theater club, even Tori's royal crew). Chrissy Lee in judge's robes—her blue hair spilling over her shoulders, lips painted red. Ben as courtroom artist, off in a corner, hunched over a giant sketchpad. Maybe even Ms. Davis as courtroom stenographer, leaning over a typewriter, revealing a bit of chest behind her floral blouse, nodding along to all my perfectly articulated arguments.

I sighed and traced the cracks in the ceiling with my eyes, finding the same face I always did in the lines. Sometimes the face winked at me, sometimes it scowled.

I wrote poetry in my head: *Unwanted memories / floated to the surface of her mind / like untethered buoys / lost at sea.*

I hadn't talked to Z since our explosion in that half-haunted garage apartment.

The moment I got to Dad's house I turned off my phone and buried it deep in my backpack. Then, as an extra safeguard against peeking, I buried my backpack deep in the hull of a random kayak gathering dust in the outdoor shed. I needed a dead zone, self-imposed. A quiet car on a teenage commuter train between now and the future. A nature reserve with ocean views.

No contact. Unreachable.

I hadn't said more than five words out loud since the afternoon at the garage apartment. I asked Dad to take me to a doctor and I was diagnosed with a viral sore throat, though I knew it wasn't a virus. My throat was red and raw from sobbing in that garage, then in the stairwell of the garage, then in Z's driveway, then on the curb waiting for a taxi to pick me up—then in the yellow taxi, then in my driveway, then in my room (at my mom), then on the open pages of my diary as I tore it from Mom's hands, then into a whole roll of toilet paper when I locked myself in the bathroom.

I'd sobbed until I was a shell of myself, a shell dissolving in my tears.

*

Dad's house was tucked off a busy main road, in a private neighborhood of New Rochelle along a wide inlet of water—which made the place feel even more ship-like. Not exactly the *sad bachelor pad* of Mom's wicked fantasies. The house was a small two-story cottage built into a hill. An exposed rock wall, bumpy with boulders, ran along one half of the inside and sweat with condensation in summer heat spells.

Dad commuted into Manhattan for work. He worked as the publisher of *The Spaces*, a posh interior design magazine, but his taste in home decor was nothing like the sparse, modern, and mostly unlivable concrete rooms that filled his glossy magazine. His house was homey and even a bit squishy—big couches, fluffy rugs, mismatched chairs, bulletin boards of postcards, piles of books, cubbies of tchotchkes.

The backyard sloped down and ended at a rock wall right before the water's edge. Every summer, the sunflowers bloomed and swayed along the side fence, heads as big as mine. Last spring, Dad and I built raised beds to grow lettuce, tomatoes, and snap peas in. The wooden boxes now were filled with compost and snow. In the winter, the house became a sanctuary for the potted plants that usually lived outside.

The snow quieted everything.

Every morning, during my retreat, Dad made us breakfast—slow-cooked oatmeal topped with blueberries, slivered almonds, a drizzle of maple syrup, and a spoonful of peanut butter. We walked our heavy bowls into the living room, balanced them in our laps, and sank into the cushioned armchairs facing the panorama window. The view was sprawling: sky, sea, tugboats, shore, snowed-in gardens, squirrels bundled in the crooks of birch branches, a ladybug wandering inside the window.

We ate and watched the birds at the feeder.

Dad taught me how to identify a Tufted Titmouse from a Dark-eyed Junco on land and a Great Blue Heron from a Snowy Egret in the water. I was fascinated by the abundance of winter ducks, some solitary, some living in teams. My favorite were the Buffleheads because of their rounded black-and-white heads, puffed up with feathers, and the way they swam in lines, neat and orderly. I imagined what duck life would be like for me, pecking and paddling beside Z and Tori, a pack of our moms splayed out to either side.

After breakfast, Dad puttered around the house, watering plants and singing along to songs in his head. Over the years, I'd shared a few Chrissy Lee albums with him. We always listened to music in the car together. Around the house, I could hear him singing one of my favorite lines: *Bad friend, stay where you are / You bring me down, you've gone too far.*

I curled up on the couch, under a grey cashmere blanket, soft as a kitten's belly.

The couch was my island. I spent all morning there, unreachable, securely and unquestionably under my blanket. Reading and writing. Thinking and dreaming.

My pile of supplies sat by my side: blank notebook, diary, the novel I was currently reading, the novel I wanted to read next, 1-3 comic books in case I wanted a graphic palette cleanser in- between reads, two pens (one black, one purple), and a full glass of water.

I stretched my legs out. I read and wrote in silence all morning.

In the afternoon, after a lunch of turkey sandwiches and potato chips, Dad always found some house project for us to do together. So far we'd: replaced the leaky u-joint under the kitchen sink, snaked out the hair clog in the bathtub (it smelled like decaying slime from the back of one million throats and looked like black sludge dredged up from an ancient lake), mounted three new bookshelves above the couch, hung up a painting using blue plastic drywall anchors, then WD-40-ed every last squeaking door hinge in the entire house.

When Dad went back to work after taking some time off to hang out with me, I had the house to myself. I'd walk laps around the cul-de-sacs, watch mollusks burp up air bubbles in the mud of low tide, write my name in the snow with a driftwood stick, collect pine-cones in the extra-deep pockets of my big pink coat, and study the evergreen moss that sleeved the trees in the backyard. I felt drained, the drafty internal storerooms of my internal life emptied. I attempted to fill them up again with trees and moss and water and birds.

I walked to the water's edge and sat on the cold rock wall, dangled my feet over the marshy water, green and murky. A fleet of seagulls floated by. On the shoreline, a Great Blue Heron stood statuesque, fishing. Low tide exposed the mucky muddy bottom, which smelled like brined fish scales and farting barnacles.

I thumbed the old lime-green lighter of Z's that lived in my coat pocket, now along with fifteen recently acquired pinecones. The lighter had no fluid left. Z dropped it one day after it failed to light a cigarette for Tori. They walked off and I scurried out from my hiding spot behind a trashcan to scoop the lighter up.

I stroked the cold plastic and fantasized about chucking the stinky thing clean across the water. Maybe it would sink and lay to rest in a muddy grave, or maybe a fish would swallow it whole, or maybe just bob and float eternally.

I jammed the lighter back into my pocket.

I didn't want to litter.

Or murder any sea-life.

As miserable as I was, I wasn't a fish-killer.

Instead, my fingers found a rough round stone from the rock wall. I held the stone high above my head and flung it as far as I could. The water swallowed the stone whole, letting out a ring of ripples.

My brother, Seth, was home from college on his winter break, too. He was supposed to be spending time at Dad's house with me, but he mostly just partied with his friends instead. He was in an endless rotating *I'm just gonna crash at a friend's house* sleepover cycle. My brother didn't like the pirate house as much as I did. I worried my dad took it personally. I know I did. I grumbled.

Right before bedtime, Z's voice barged back into my mind. In the dark it was harder to see her coming.

Most nights, I rocked myself to sleep with Chrissy Lee singing in my headphones. *You had my heart / you had me / I was your art / can't you see?*

I set sail on my ship and bathed in the silence of the stars.

*

Ever since our poetry unit in Ms. Davis' class, I'd been reading all the poetry I could get my hands on. Meanwhile, I started crafting poems in my head. As I read, I catalogued the poems I wanted to write—was too afraid to write.

It wasn't until winter break at Dad's house that I finally put pen to paper.

I filled page after page.

I felt lighter as my notebook grew heavy with ink.

*

One morning, I found Dad hunched over the kitchen table, a small cactus in a terra-cotta pot sat in front of him. He held a pair of tweezers in each hand and peered through the smudged reading glasses perched on the tip of his nose. Tied across his forehead was a folded-up red bandana, a faded relic from his hippie days. The sleeves of his beige cable-knit sweater were pushed up past his elbows. His thinning hair was gray and short but not bristly. His beard, full but trimmed.

"Hey, Nattie," he said. Dad was the only person to consistently use my childhood nickname, but I didn't mind. From him, it felt like sipping hot soup on a cold day. I sat down next to Dad, scooting my chair closer to see what he was doing. He continued with his task, wordlessly.

I sat in the quiet with him.

I watched as he pulled tiny black seeds from the flowers of the cactus with the careful precision of a surgeon. They looked like poppy-seeds—dark, round, and impossibly small. Hard to imagine that a cactus could grow from something so tiny, so easily squished. I offered up a cupped hand and Dad dropped the excavated seeds into my palm one by one for safe keeping. We sat very still and made a good team.

"Mom tells me you got into a fight with Z," Dad said, dropping another seed into my hand.

I nodded. The seed rolled, following the love line of my palm. I hated that I knew about love lines. Months ago, I overheard Tori explaining palmistry to Z. I hated the memory of Tori caressing Z's hand, kissing all the lines as she named them.

"I'm sorry, Nattie. Do you want to talk about it?"
"Not really," I said.
"No problem."
"But did Mom tell you what she did afterwards?"
He shook his head.
"It was awful, Dad."
"What happened?"
"Mom—"
My throat was dry. I needed water.
"What?" He paused, tweezers in mid-squeeze.
"She read my diary."
"Your diary?"
"She read all my private thoughts."
"What?" he asked again.
"I know."
"Wow."

"She told me it was an accident, that she was only in my room to make my bed and that somehow my notebook got knocked off the bedside table, fell open, and she just happened to read it as she put it back. But *I* make my bed, every day. She doesn't do that. Ever. She just marched into my room and read my private journal."

I stopped myself. I was talking a lot. I hadn't said this many words out loud in weeks, maybe even years.

Dad was listening. "What did you do?"
"Ran to the bathroom, slammed the door."
"Did Mom try to come in?"
"I sat with my back against the door."

My thighs tensed up remembering how hard I pressed my whole body against the wood, bracing myself, and even still Mom tried to open the door.

"She kept asking me questions through the door," I said.
"You didn't want to talk."
"I said leave me alone, go away, leave me alone."
Dad was quiet. "I'm sorry she did that," he said.

We turned back to the cactus and reentered the quiet meditation of seed-hunting.

I wanted that night out of my body, out of my mind. The double betrayal, first Z, then Mom—

The seeds pooled together in the cup of my hand.

"Well I think that's all of them," Dad said. "Want to help me replant some of these later?"

"Sure."

"I've been saving a green pot just for you. We can plant a seed in there for you to take back to Mom's with you."

His smile was wide and tender.

"Thanks." I smiled back.

We returned to our quiet.

Chapter 20: The Equation

The next morning, Dad stood at the kitchen island readying my cactus seed for transit, nestling the painted green pot into a grocery bag and swaddling it with crumpled newspaper.

"Your mom will be here in five," Dad said, glancing up.

"Okay," I said, my backpack and suitcase already by the front door. I had yet to turn my phone back on. For the first time ever, I'd let my parents negotiate the terms of my transfer, unmoderated.

I stood at the living room window, staring out across the water, finding that spot where sea and sky become one, blues blending and colliding. In my last quiet moments, I practiced embodying the calm of high tide: shoulders down, jaw loose, stomach unknotted, feet planted.

The *scrunch, scrunch, scrunch* of the gravel driveway signaled Mom's arrival.

My retreat was over.

"She's here," I said more to myself than to anyone else.

Dad carried my bags to the car. I followed him out of the pirate house. Mom stood up out of her seat but kept one foot firmly grounded on the car floor, half-in, half-out. She used the door as a shield, holding it between her and Dad.

"Hi Deborah," Dad said, clicking the trunk shut.

"Caleb," Mom gave him a formal nod.

I hugged Dad. Mom stared at us.

"I had the best time," I whispered to him.

Dad squeezed me tight and whispered back: "It'll be okay."

I took a breath before descending into Mom's car. I buckled in, grasping the bagged plant in my lap for dear life.

Great Dismal Swamp

Faith Shearin

All the women on my mother's side of the family are widows. There are no men. Or, rather, the men are temporary. They are bitten by snakes in tropical jungles or drowned by rogue waves while surfing. They are struck by lightning while playing golf, or attacked by wild dogs, or stung by jellyfish. My father, Sebastian Strand, was a traveling salesman who fell asleep at the wheel on a long drive home, and steered his car over a guard rail into the afterlife. Sometimes, in dreams, I still find him motoring through a dark swamp. This was May 13 of 1985, when I was twelve years old and my brother, Liam, was fifteen. Shortly after this, our mother, Rosemary, sold our rickety farmhouse in the Pioneer Valley of Massachusetts and moved us into our Grandma Harriet Firth's cottage by the sea.

Grandma Firth lived on the island of Ocracoke, off the coast of North Carolina, in a fishing village where certain ancient villagers still spoke with an accent British settlers left behind. (Grandma called this the High Tide Accent and it was full of long vowels and extra syllables.) Her cottage could only be reached by ferry and—after we pulled away from the dock—our mother showed Liam and me how to feed stale crackers and bread to the seagulls flapping overhead. I liked the way they flew close and tugged the bread from my hand while the water behind us whitened. We had only visited Grandma Firth a half dozen times during my childhood, and three of those visits took place while I was still a baby, so Liam and I didn't know her very well. I suppose I knew there were secrets on my mother's side of the family: legacies hidden by sand dunes and the endless beating of the sea. I knew there was something my mother hoped to escape by moving inland with our father, who arrived on Ocracoke to sell pharmaceuticals to the island's only physician, Doctor Halloran, the June after she'd graduated from college. Our mother, Rosemary, was the receptionist in Halloran's office that summer, a job that caused her to catch Strep Throat, Pink Eye, Whooping Cough, and Slap Cheek, and—after giving his sales pitch—our father asked her to go to lunch with him at The Pony Island Restaurant, where she ordered the flounder, and he ordered a hamburger with extra pickles and, by July, he had driven her away from her family and settled her on his grandparents' Amherst valley farmland, among chickens and bearded goats. I grew up away from the ocean though my name, Maris, means of the sea.

Liam and I were glad to leave Amherst because we were tired of being pitied by our teachers and classmates. We were sick of the way women appeared on our doorstep with casseroles and spoke to us slowly, in hushed voices, as if grief had made us stupid. We hated the stiff, fragrant flower arrangements on our porch, and the sympathy cards that arrived in pastel envelopes, saying things like: *Thinking of you at this difficult time* or *Sometimes there are no words.* Our mother had been a housewife until our father died; then, she became a woman who delivered death certificates to car dealerships and phone companies. Sometimes, Liam and I accompanied her on these errands, where we watched sweaty, middle aged men in cubicles mop their foreheads, apologize, and search for a manager. Rosemary stopped cooking dinner after our father died, and ate most of her meals standing over our kitchen sink, where she consumed cold things from cans: tuna, usually, or pineapple packed in its own juice. I listened to her slurping the juice.

Liam and I learned to make our own dinners. We favored spaghetti (Liam knew how to boil noodles) and baked beans (I could open the can) but we also ate frozen TV dinners: the kind that had little compartments for the meat, potato, and vegetable. When we dined, we balanced our plates on the coffee table, and pretended to watch reruns of MASH or Gilligan's Island on the TV in the living room, while listening to our mother cry and talk on the phone with Grandma Firth or her younger sister, Hali. We peered through the living room doorway into the kitchen, where she sat at a table, cradling the phone against one shoulder, and fiddling with the long, curly cord. Our mother had always been pretty in an understated way; she had bobbed brown hair, blue eyes, and freckles, but becoming a widow had left her thin and faded.

"I told the lady in the social security office that I'm a housewife," our mother said, "and she pointed out that you can't really *be* a housewife if your husband is dead, can you? So, I guess I'm unemployed."

It was during one of these phone calls that we learned our father had died without life insurance, and the only money our mother could cobble together would come from selling our ramshackle farmhouse. This is how we came to know the realtor, Tiffany, who balanced on high heels in our driveway while chickens darted in front of her, and a bearded goat nibbled the skirt of her pink business suit. Liam and I watched Tiffany drift through all the drafty rooms of our farmhouse with our mother, deciding on the best way to describe the place.

"We'll say it has old fashioned charm," Tiffany said. She pulled a lipstick from her purse and dotted her upper lip; then, she pressed her lips together.

Our father's side of the family, the Strands, had never liked our mother and they weren't happy with her for selling a house and farmland that had been in their family since the late 1800s. They came—just before we packed our van for the long drive to North Carolina—to go through our father's belongings: Grandma Dolores Strand, whose mouth was naturally turned down in a permanent frown, and our father's siblings, Oliver and Samantha, who worked as actuaries under fluorescent lights, which had leeched all color from their skin.

"Your father's death was statistically improbable," Samantha told me. She was out of breath from climbing the stairs and she was packing up his typewriter and ties. She kept a tissue tucked up one sleeve of her oversized dress so she could regularly wipe her eyes.

"Your mother should have gotten a job and kept this land," Grandma Strand told me while packing up the frying pan she'd given our parents as a wedding gift.

Our mother had gone for a walk in the park so our father's family could take whatever they wanted. "We don't have room for it at Grandma Firth's cottage anyway," she had pointed out. Still, Liam and I didn't like the way Grandma Strand, Oliver, and Samantha were dismantling what remained of our father. They gathered around our father's belongings the way vultures might gather over a deceased squirrel. I watched them fill the back of their station wagon with boxes.

They took a trophy our father had won for running cross country in high school in the Northeast Kingdom of

Vermont, where he had jogged on snowy roads, his breath ethereal. They took a book of Raymond Carver short stories he had dog-eared called *What We Talk About When We Talk About Love*. They took the tins of Altoids peppermints he carried in his suit pockets. They took his Bob Dylan records: *Blood on the Tracks* and *Blonde on Blonde*.

The truth was that Liam and I had grown used to our father coming and going so he didn't seem *dead* to us yet. We were still waiting for his headlights to pierce the darkness, for the sound of his Ford Escort purring in the driveway. We were waiting for him to open his suitcase and give us the gifts he had collected in distant towns: cowboy hats, t-shirts, chocolate bars, kites, ice skates, mugs, stuffed snakes.

Ocracoke Island was a sandy, windblown place, where salt-worn cottages had wraparound porches or stood on stilts, and Grandma Firth's bungalow was on Lighthouse Road, near an ivory lighthouse that guarded an inlet. She lived among fishermen whose yards were stacked high with crab pots, buoys, shad boats, and fishing nets. As soon as Liam and I slipped out of our van, I was overcome by the presence of the sea. I breathed the salt of it, heard its restless reaching.

Grandma Harriet Firth was sitting in a rocking chair on her front porch with her overfed chihuahua, Sugar, who balanced his girth over miniature stick legs. He had ears that stood up and bulging eyes that made him appear eternally surprised. Our mother opened the van door and ran to Grandma, and Liam and I stood, stunned, in the sandy yard, beneath the gnarled southern live oaks, watching our mother wrap her arms around Grandma Harriet, and weep on her shoulder. Sugar balanced on top of a wicker chair and barked a bark that seemed to announce our arrival; it was a bark that required the effort of his entire diminutive body. Aunt Hali opened a screen door and ran out to hug Liam and me. Hali was four years younger than our mother, and her brown hair was curly. She wore a gauzy sundress and smelled like shampoo and coconut oil.

"Ya'll must be so tired," she said.

"Come on up here," Grandma Firth called to us and we climbed the stairs to her wide front porch which was cluttered with chairs, shells, and books. Two hammocks hung at either end and swayed in the breeze. Our mother stepped aside, so Grandma Firth could hug Liam and me at the same time, pulling our heads towards her enormous bosom. Grandma wore a blue floral housedress and she was barefoot. I would learn that she loved the color blue -- all the walls of her cottage were awash in it—and I would learn that she loved baking: her kitchen counter eternally dusted with flour and sugar.

"Hali," Grandma Firth said, "get these children some chocolate chip cookies."

The cookies, which were brought to Liam and me on a blue tin plate with matching mugs of milk, tasted better than anything we'd eaten since our father died. Grief—Liam and I were learning—altered the taste of food. Liam and my mother and I all lacked appetite. We ate half of what we'd eaten before, and sometimes forgot lunch altogether. Whenever I ate I was aware of our father in the swamp of his afterlife, eating nothing. Grandma Firth's cookies had some intoxicating combination of chocolate chips, vanilla extract, and eggs and—when I dipped them in milk—they tasted like the Saturday mornings when Liam and I were small and we were allowed to help ourselves to bowls and bowls of sugary cereal and watch cartoons while our parents slept late.

We watched Scooby Doo and Shaggy wander through haunted mansions in search of cobwebbed kitchens and we watched Wilma and Fred Flintstone use their bare feet to propel their Stone Age automobile; we watched the Pink Panther outwit a pale, dogged inspector with a pointy face to the sound of a joyous jazz saxophone. By the time we were watching *The Pink Panther*, our father woke up and wandered downstairs in his plaid pajamas, his black curly hair tall and unruly. He danced his way to the kitchen, where he brewed coffee, unrolled the newspaper, and began cracking eggs.

Our mother had always been bookish and—while I was unpacking my suitcases at Grandma's house—I began to understand why: the Firth house was heavy with books. There were crowded bookshelves in the living room and kitchen, packed bookshelves in hallways, and baskets filled with books in both bathrooms. Liam and I were given matching attic bedrooms with low, slanted ceilings, and futons on the floor, and some of Grandma's books had made their way upstairs. We found them stacked against our bedroom walls in precarious columns that collapsed whenever a strong wind breathed through our opened windows. (The books in my room were mysteries and I began reading my way through them: Agatha Christie's *And Then There Were None*, *Harriet the Spy* and hardcover Nancy Drews that smelled like some dusty, rainy afternoon in the past.) Grandma Firth ran a cluttered bookshop on School Street, and she accepted donations of used books that were sometimes delivered to her house instead of her store, and these books tended to linger on her porch. Some that she found interesting (and Grandma had many interests, including skin diseases, pirates, shipwrecks, and obscure plagues) found their way upstairs. She wore her reading glasses around her neck and read while cooking, or before napping, or while walking down the sandy, tree-lined streets. Rosemary had inherited this habit from Harriet. All through our childhoods, Liam and I found our mother behind a book. She was fond of poetry, in particular, and took us, when we were small, to roam around the house and gardens of the late poet Emily Dickinson. There were pictures of Liam and me sitting on the porch of Emily's two-story Amherst house, where our mother read aloud to us: "I dwell in possibility— A fairer House than Prose—More numerous of Windows— Superior—for Doors…"

When our grade school classes toured Emily's homestead Liam and I impressed our teachers with facts about the poet. We knew, for instance, that her dog had been named Carlo, and that she liked to bake bread but disliked housework. We knew that Emily played piano, wore a white dress, and did not marry, that she had an herbarium, and enjoyed pressing flowers into letters and books. Our mother told us that this impulse to preserve something temporary and beguiling like a flower—by pressing it to paper—was like the impulse to write a poem. Rosemary carried around a collection of notebooks into which she scrawled things: memories, notes, ideas for song lyrics, poems she sometimes read aloud to Liam and me.

Our first afternoon on the island Aunt Hali took Liam and me to the beach. We brought Sugar with us and rode in Hali's jeep which had towels, beach chairs, buckets, and shovels packed in the back. It was a fine June day: dappled light, the clouds light and high. Hali showed us how to hike through a low place between sand dunes, among whispering beach grasses, to a glittering white shore. Sugar trotted confidently, leading the way. Once we settled on a spot—between a sunburned fisherman casting his line into the surf, and an old woman with a wide- brimmed hat collecting driftwood—Sugar dug a hole with his twiggy legs and nestled in the darker, cooler sand, panting, and I opened a *People* magazine I'd bought in a 7-11 before we left Amherst. After our father died I had begun reading about rich and famous people. I liked to read about Princess Diana's sapphire engagement ring, for instance, and her wedding at which she had worn a taffeta gown covered in ten thousand pearls, and her silk shoes embroidered with more than five hundred sequins; I liked reading about Carrie Fisher's braids and golden bikini in *Return of the Jedi* and looking at pictures of the mansion where she had grown up with her movie star mother, Debbie Reynolds. I enjoyed imagining the lives of people who had twenty-three wedding cakes, and did not have dead fathers, and did not need to sell their farmhouses. I tried to imagine what it would be like to be rich and wake up in a king-sized bed and float in my own private swimming pool with a waterfall and eat pastries delivered from Paris.

Liam and Hali walked down to the surf and I watched them wading in the froth of crashing waves where leggy shorebirds with thin beaks hurried forwards and backwards. A crab with splendid pincers drifted up from an underworld near my foot, flinging sand, and Sugar barked at it.

"Maris," Liam called to me, his voice small against the wind and surf, "there are sand dollars."

I placed a conch shell on top of my magazine, to keep it from blowing away, and wandered down to the mouth of the ocean, where I felt something strange and new. My feet rubbed against the rough fragments of shell—which reminded me of miniature ears or polished turrets—and my breathing and heart recognized the regular crash of the waves, and my skin tingled in the cool salt air, and—though we had just moved to Ocracoke—I felt I had come home.

Grandma Firth had a meeting of her book group for widows the first Saturday after our arrival. She held the gathering on her front porch where she arranged a platter of fruit, cheese, and crackers on a side table, beside a plate of chocolate chip cookies. I liked watching her traipse around the kitchen, getting ready, while Billy Joel sang "Uptown Girl" on the radio. Grandma believed in making a mess when she cooked. Sugar travelled at her heels, his bulging eyes alert, dining on whatever fell. After each meal she abandoned a sink full of dishes that floated lazily in brackish water.

"Should I wash these?" I asked one morning, after pancakes.

"You can wash them if you like, honey, but there's no hurry," Grandma said. "They're soaking."

"What does soaking do?" I asked.

"Have you ever watched sheets fluttering on a laundry line?" Grandma asked.

"Yes," I said.

"Soaking dishes makes me feel like that," Grandma said. I had no idea what she was talking about.

Grandma Firth didn't mind if she got flour all over her hands or if it dusted the skirt of her dress. She had a glass punch bowl and she showed me how to mix ginger ale with cranberry juice and slice lemons and oranges thinly and float them on top like rafts in a great burgundy sea; then, Mom, Grandma, Liam and I sat in wicker chairs, in the twilight, waiting.

"It's my favorite time of day," Grandma said.

"Why?" Liam asked.

"The whole street turns blue and—just for a moment—everything loses its shadow," Grandma said.

I stared out at the darkening wax myrtles, salt-stunted cedars, and twisted oaks. I saw the other cottages sinking into night and they looked as if they might be under water. The children across the street drifted back and forth in a drowned tire swing, two fishermen floated in a yard to the east, mending black nets, and even the white lighthouse looked submerged. Beyond our neighborhood there were salt marshes and sand flats, the plains of grasses cut by winding creeks, and I imagined night enveloping them too, like a high tide.

Four women came to book group: Nancy, whose husband had died of a heart attack while dancing on a yacht; Linda, whose husband had died of a pernicious skin cancer that expanded over his back and arms; Susan, who was ninety, and whose husband had forgotten everything, even his own name, then wandered into the sea; and Jackie, whose husband was killed in a hunting accident, by a friend who mistook him for a bird. I could tell these women already knew the story of our father because they nodded at my mother, and Liam, and me the way you might nod at a fellow passenger on a sinking ship. The book they were discussing was *Jonathan Livingston Seagull* and, as far as I could tell, the story was about a seagull who was a misfit because he wanted to perfect his flying instead of squabbling over food.

"I like the part where, in his old age, he is met by two radiant seagulls," Nancy said, "and he learns that his body is nothing more than thought itself."

"I liked Chiang," Linda said, "who tells Jonathan to keep working on love."

"I thought the whole thing was nonsense," Susan said.

"Why?" Grandma asked her.

"It doesn't matter if Jonathan focuses on finding food or flying," Susan pointed out, "or if he believes his body is thought, or bones and feathers, or dust, he's still going to *die*."

"But won't his life have been more meaningful?" Jackie asked.

"Every life is meaningful," our mother said.

"True," Susan said. She was eating a cheese cracker and Sugar had positioned himself at the base of her wicker chair, awaiting crumbs.

"I'm not sure widows need to read a book like this," Grandma Firth said, "We already know that life is short and petty things don't matter."

"Is there a name for a child with one dead parent?" I asked. I blushed when all the women turned to look at me.

"There should be a name for that," Nancy said, "but I can't think of what it is."

"Unlucky," Linda suggested.

"We're half orphans," Liam said, and he winked at me.

"I suppose you are," Grandma said.

I could tell our mother was worried about money because I found her asleep with a notebook full of numbers opened over her chest. I discovered her half full cups of Earl Grey tea growing cold around the cottage: on the living room coffee table, on the kitchen counter, on a shelf in the bathroom. Each one rested on top of a folded piece of paper on which sums had been subtracted from other sums in red pen. I knew our mother disliked math, and claimed to be bad at it, (she had always refused to help Liam with his algebra homework, telling him to ask our father instead) so I knew she wasn't adding and subtracting for fun.

"Do you think we're poor?" I asked Liam one night when we were alone. We often spoke to each other through the thin dividing wall between our rooms, while reclining in our attic beds, but—if we weren't sleepy—I liked to sit at the edge of his futon and watch him sketch. Liam had always been able to draw. He pressed a pencil to paper and vivid, moody scenes emerged. He was busily sketching a floor lamp with a cylindrical shade, which stood pensively in the corner of his room.

"We're poor," Liam said, "I just asked Aunt Hali if I could bus tables at her restaurant."

"Do you think I could get a job?" I asked.

"You're too young," Liam said.

"Maybe I could babysit," I said.

"You hate children," Liam reminded me.

I had begun noticing fathers. Whenever Grandma took me with her to her bookshop, *The Castaway*, to unpack boxes of used books and pick out a few to take home with me, I saw tourist fathers buying books for their daughters. I pretended to be lost in my Nancy Drew mystery but I was really watching the girls my own age. I saw how their fathers followed them protectively around the store; I noticed the way their fathers touched their hair affectionately. I saw fathers pull out their wallets and buy their daughters Judy Blume novels, or Mad Libs, or sunglasses. Nancy Drew was a half orphan like me but even she had a father: a handsome attorney named Carson Drew who encouraged her to be a detective.

At Aunt Hali's restaurant, *Queen Anne's Revenge*, where she tended bar—and Liam and I were allowed to eat free grilled cheese sandwiches on Mondays when things were slow—I saw ordinary families arrive for lunch: two parents, two kids. They sat in booths, and the kids colored in the sea horses on their placemats, or dipped their french fries in puddles of ketchup, while the parents laughed and held hands. When Liam and I went to the beach with Aunt Hali and her long-haired boyfriend, Jerome, we saw fathers teaching their sons and daughters how to fish or surf. We watched, spellbound, as fathers stood behind their children, showing them how to cast lines into the sea; we watched as fathers taught their children to balance on cresting waves. Once, on School Street, a girl named Jan stopped by on her bicycle and invited me to her cottage, where we spent an afternoon dressing up as Blackbeard: the pirate who lived on Ocracoke in the early 1700s. Jan had a closet full of costumes and we tied ribbons onto black wigs and wore vests and captain's hats and went into her back yard to stand in one of her father's abandoned skiffs, where we pretended to rule the high seas. I was happy until we were called in to dinner, and her father, Billy Dunbar, made her a hamburger just the way she liked it. He asked what I wanted on mine, and I said mayonnaise and pickles—which was the way my father had taught me to eat hamburgers—and then, when he put the burger on my plate, I found I couldn't eat it.

I began keeping a notebook like the detectives in the novels I read in my attic bedroom at night. When I couldn't sleep, I slipped downstairs, sat on the porch, and wrote in my notebook and listened to the sea. I removed a single chocolate chip cookie from Grandma's jar on the kitchen counter and ate it slowly, with my eyes closed, pretending someone else was feeding me. On one of those late night rambles I snuck into Grandma's bedroom to borrow a jacket and found her bed empty and her window wide open, her gauzy curtains billowing. There was water on her floor and a pair of men's Wellingtons. Grandma had been a widow since 1965, when her husband, Jack, disappeared in his fishing trawler during a nor'easter, so I didn't know why a man's boots waited beside her bed. I noticed other things too: the way Grandma and the other widows from her book group liked to go to the sea at twilight, with baskets, buckets, and wine, and did not return until the wee hours of the morning. I asked my mother about this once—when she was reclined on a hammock with a washcloth over her forehead—and she told me Grandma had always been wild and sleepless.

"She just enjoys collecting shells with her friends," my mother said, gesturing around her at the sandy piles of Scotch Bonnets, Whelks, Moon Snails, and Augers stacked on the porch stairs and railing. "It's not much of a mystery."

Liam had been working as a bus boy for about a week when I found my job as a babysitter. I'd been sorting books with Grandma Firth at *The Castaway* when a willowy woman chased a toddler named Caspian through the front door of the shop. I learned his name right away because his mother said it every few seconds.

"Caspian, *no*" she said, or "Caspian, don't touch that." Caspian didn't seem to hear her.

We'd brought Sugar with us, and he was asleep at my feet, and I was sorting books that had been salvaged from a dead woman's house. The woman had collected books about mythic sea creatures, and books about the glamorous lives of the Kennedys; she had collected books about famous shipwrecks and lost treasures. I found myself setting aside a few heavy tomes to carry up to my attic. I was busy studying a picture of a mythic Kraken—which could toss ships into the air with its many long arms—when I heard Sugar growling and I saw Caspian reaching for him with one sticky hand.

"Caspian, no! Don't bother the doggy!" his mother cried. She was running across the store to grab him but I had already distracted him by showing him the picture of the Kraken. Caspian liked the drawing of the giant octopus holding a ship aloft in a sea full of white caps and he instantly forgot about Sugar, sat down, and stuck his thumb in his mouth. He sat perfectly still while I read to him about the cephalopod's arms pulling sailors to the bottom of the sea.

"Do you babysit?" the mother asked me.

"Can I, Grandma?" I asked.

After this, twice a week, I walked four streets over to Curiosity Lane, to a beach box on stilts, and babysat for Caspian while his mother, Heather, worked as a tour guide at The Blackbeard Museum.

"He loves to go to the beach," Heather said on my first visit, pointing to a wagon full of buckets and shovels. "Just watch him carefully. Make sure he doesn't wade out too far."

"Do you have a favorite fact about Blackbeard?" I asked.

"Well, he married a local girl named Mary," Heather said, "and they had a daughter, Elizabeth. Some say she died and some say she didn't."

"So he might have great grandchildren?" I asked.

"It's possible." Heather said. She leaned her head forward to brush her hair into a ponytail.

The only thing I'd learned about Blackbeard back in Amherst was that he'd been attacked by a navy force from Virginia that arrived in sloops designed to navigate the shallow, twisting channels around Ocracoke. They had slayed him with gunshots and swords, and cut off his head—placing it on a bowsprit to carry away—but, according to my teacher—there were mythic tales about how his headless body had gone on swimming in the murky waters of the Pamlico Sound. I dreamed about this and, in the dream, Blackbeard's blind, headless body swam arm over arm until he reached the swamp where my father's car idled among bald cypress trees.

Just after my father died, I had read a police report that included a description of the place where he had driven into the afterlife: outside a town called Elizabeth City, on a lonely road that stretched through the Great Dismal Swamp. This was a remote swamp where Native American tribes had once fled the colonial frontier, a place where escaped slaves had hidden from captors. In an encyclopedia in Grandma Firth's bookshop I read that runaways had built shacks there, cleared small fields, and subsisted on corn, hogs, and chickens, keeping to higher ground. I liked reading about the swamp's tupelo trees, bobcats, otters, weasels, and alligators; I imagined that my father's spirit wandered out of his wrecked car and discovered a shack and I imagined he waited for me there, in a forest damp with secrets.

The Path of the Sun

Lauren Goodsmith

The Road of Hope (1984)

Emory pressed her palms against the bone-white sand, scalding, soft as ash. She let her fingers sink down to find silty coolness, unexpected and sweet, just beneath the surface. When she closed her fists around the powder-fine grains, they escaped her grasp.

She looked up, feeling a gaze upon her, and met the look of the woman in the lime-green *melafah*. She was resting sideways in the shade of the bush-taxi, easy and recumbent, propped by an angled elbow. A gauzy fold of cloth covered the lower part of her face, a filter against the dust, as she regarded the lanky *nasraniyya* who liked to play with sand in the sun of midday.

Emory smiled. "*Hami hatta,*" she said, very hot, and immediately felt foolish.

"*Wellahi,*" replied the woman. Indeed. With a brief glottal cluck, she drew her *melafah* over her head and nestled into the crook of her arm to doze.

Clearly there had been little progress. The ancient Peugeot's hood still gaped, the head and shoulders of the driver still hunched over its innards. Three of the passengers, Ray-Banned white Moors who had purchased the prime front seats, stood around him, their blue robes rippling in the dry wind. One of them muttered at the man's bent back and cast his cigarette stub into the dunes with disgust. The driver raised his head for air and drew an arm across his dark, sweat-soaked face.

The other passengers nestled in the taxi's trapezoid shadow, Carmen among them, deep in her dog-eared copy of Where There Is No Doctor. Six months in Mauritania and already showing the *sangfroid* of an old hand.

Emory stood and squinted against the tinny glare. The ribbon of road stretched out taut in either direction before dissolving in a shimmer of heat-haze. More than once during their trip, the highway's habit of melting away before and behind them had given her the unsettling sense that it existed for only small, marginally navigable snatches at a time.

A blur appeared, and the air carried the cough of another overtaxed engine. Emory watched as the shape materialized into a bush-taxi like their own, but with its roof piled impossibly high with boxes, burlap sacks, jerry-cans, rolled mats and rugs, all secured by a crosshatching of ropes. As it neared, the taxi curved wide to avoid a dune that had seeped onto the roadway. The maneuver set its load swaying perilously, and the car slowed to regain equilibrium.

"God knows where they'll go," said Carmen, suddenly at her side. Beneath her blue "STAMP OUT MALARIA" cap, her cheeks were rosy in the heat. "They told us in training that something like twenty thousand have arrived in Nouakchott already. And that's just since January."

As the bush-taxi faltered past, Emory glimpsed the figures in the rear seat: a gaunt-faced man and woman, two thin children pressed between them, another clutched in the woman's lap.

The bush-taxi tottered off, leaving a rank diesel plume in its wake. Emory coughed, and Carmen passed her the canteen.

"Thanks." Emory took a swig. The metal was warm, the water long gone tepid. They stared after the retreating taxi.

"Are you sure they're headed to the city?" asked Emory. "Could they maybe stop at one of the towns before that, somewhere along the road that's received supplies, and wait it out there?"

"Hah. They could try, but from what I've heard, the chances aren't very good. Not much actually getting out to the interior stations, apparently."

"But what about all those WFP trucks we saw being loaded up? Where were they going to?"

"Yes, well, some of them head out to the regional capitals where, in theory, the stocks get divvied up to be sent to the depots and distribution sites. But seems there's pretty major skimming all along the way, so what's left is barely enough for the locals, much less any new arrivals."

"But who's taking it? How does that happen?"

Carmen pushed back the brim of her cap and wiped her forehead. "Whoever manages to make a deal with someone along the way, I guess, or spirit away some sacks between weigh-stations." She gave a dry laugh. "Local version of trickle-down economics."

Emory stared at her. "But that's awful. Why are they getting away with it? Can't there be someone monitoring the loads, making sure they're not tampered with?"

"So you'd think," said Carmen. "But apparently that very sensible measure is not yet fully in place. Meantime, the Route D'Espoir is a very long one, and far more twisty than it looks."

Emory looked again after the retreating *taxi-brousse*, now a smudge at the horizon's edge. Although she and Carmen had spent only a couple of days in the capital before heading into the interior, she'd seen them everywhere—

refugees from the drought in the interior, squatting under improvised shelters along the road or sitting and waiting with vacant eyes under the scant shade of the trees that lined the drive outside the UN compound. She could not begin to imagine what this family would find at the end of their journey, and only hoped that it would at least be something more than what they'd left behind.

The stalled progress of their own trip had stirred her to restlessness, heightened now by a sense of frustration. She turned away from the road, looking towards the low dunes beyond the ailing Peugeot. "I think I'll stretch my legs a little."

"Okay, only don't wander too far. And steer clear of scorpions." Carmen settled back by the taxi and riffled the pages of her book. "I haven't gotten to that part yet."

Emory headed towards the nearest sandy rise, the tail of which already gently brushed the asphalt. It was a small dune, compared with some they'd seen during their drive eastward from Aleg—great crescents that caught golden shadows in their folds and seemed to go on forever. She climbed slowly, feeling the pull in her calves, letting her feet sink deep into the powder-fine drift.

Her legs, after so many hours in the crowded taxi, were glad of their freedom. They propelled her over another rise and across a broad, stony space studded with bits of flint and shale. A pair of meager thorn-bushes bristled between two large rocks, and she noted them as way-markers. Soon after, a slight descent, and the ground softened and striated into low ripples like the bottom of a desiccated lake. Halfway across the depression, she slowed in surprise. From one edge of the pan to the other, the color of the sand seemed to shift, from palest ivory to warm amber. Backtracking, she studied the gradation—subtle but definite, no trick of the light. She straightened with a laugh, a little breathless now, and went on.

Carmen's call had come out of the blue. "Come on out, come visit before I get medevacked for malaria or schisto or who knows what. You could use a break, right? And where better than what's basically the world's biggest beach?"

Which they never actually went to. The currents along the four-hundred-mile coastline, roiling and notorious, deterred all but the hardiest swimmers, and to sunbathe in the Saharan heat would be madness. They did visit the fishmarket along the shore, raucous with the cries of the Wolof vendors, alive with the gleam of dorade and *thioff* pulled fresh from the nets of the dancing wooden boats.

After two nights spent in the sprawling capital with the wondrously hospitable Dieyé family, Carmen's hosts during her Peace Corps training, they traveled south by bush-taxi to the tiny, thatch-roofed village where she'd been assigned as a health aide. Along the way, Emory watched the dunes give grudging way to scrawny foliage, then flatten out into savannah. In the river valley the transformation became complete, and they seemed to be in a different country. Vegetable gardens bounded the neat mudbrick homes, sorghum fringed the silt-red shore, and the cornfields of Senegal gleamed on the far bank. During their return northward, the progression reversed itself, the desert gradually reclaiming the land once more, its emptiness unbroken except for sudden stark clusters of rock and the occasional acacia or palm. Or by the furtive peak of a tent, barely glimpsed before it melted away, mirage-like, amid the vastness of the sands.

Another dune now presented itself, honey hued, broader than it was high. Emory labored up the soft slope, panting as she reached the summit, slid down the far side, and stopped.

Before her was a small, brown tent, its sides sloping winglike from a sharp pinnacle. A woman was there, with a child beside her and a baby, naked, crawling unsteadily over the woven mat that covered the sand.

The tent was pitched in a flat, pebble-strewn area between the swells of the surrounding dunes, not a hundred yards from the road. They were close enough to hear the voices of the men, raised high in debate over the engine's malady, carried in ragged snatches by the wind.

Emory and the woman stared at one another, speechless. The older child, a thin, solemn-faced boy of six or seven, let out a short exclamation. The baby began to snuffle and the woman lifted it into her lap, wiping its runny nose with a corner of her frayed *melafah*. Then she looked up.

"*Assalaamu 'aleykum.*" Her voice was shorn, slightly rasping, as if long unused.

"*W'aleykum assalaam,*" said Emory.

"*Tfaddal.*" The woman motioned for Emory to sit down, the movement of her arm hampered by the infant, who was now clutching tightly at the folds of her robe.

Emory nodded. She moved into the tent's dusky shade and sat at the edge of the woven mat. The older child still stared at her, his black eyes fastened on her hair, pulled carelessly back at the nape.

"*Shoukran,*" said Emory to the woman. Thank you. To the watchful boy she gave a smile.

Her thoughts meantime tumbled over one another. She'd fast discovered that the standard Arabic of her college courses was alien to native ears. Although basic grammar and syntax were mostly the same, the dialect here was dense with odd inflections and Berber-based words. Concentrating hard, she could usually understand two-thirds of what was being said; the rest disappeared into a tangle of rapid-fire idioms and glottal stops. Now she groped for local phrases she'd tried to absorb over the past few days.

She gestured over her shoulder. "*Ana asafir—f'il share'*," she said slowly. I'm traveling. On the road.

The woman nodded. "*Shor Nouakchott?*"

"*Aywa. Laken fi mushkila...*" But the car has a problem, so we're waiting for it to be fixed.

The woman nodded again. "*Insh'allah.*"

Emory tried to calm the pulse in her ears and cobble together some more words that would make sense. Her tongue felt awkward, too large, and her mouth dust-dry. Into the silence the woman spoke in a low voice to the boy. He picked up a chipped wooden bowl and disappeared behind the tent.

Emory made another attempt. "And you...you are traveling somewhere? Or staying here?"

"We are also going to the city. We wait here for my husband to return." The infant squirmed and fretted in the woman's arms. "He will come with people in a truck or a car, after trading with them. Then we will go."

"To Nouakchott?"

"*Aywa.*" Yes.

The flatness of her tone momentarily halted the exchange. In the space of this new, more natural pause, Emory realized that she had understood everything the woman had said. She spoke again, slowly. "And how long have you been waiting here for him?"

"*Tlaat dushur.*" Three months.

The boy reappeared silently, and at a word from the woman placed in Emory's hands the wooden bowl, now filled with brownish liquid. "Thank you," said Emory. It came out like a croak: "*Shoukran.*" The boy nodded once, sat down beside his mother, and continued to stare with onyx eyes.

Emory lifted the bowl to her lips. She hesitated an instant, then drank. At first she tasted nothing, just felt the cool rush against her tongue, down her dry throat. Then she was drinking deeply, greedily. She'd had no idea how thirsty she was. It was cold, slightly malty, indescribably refreshing. The wooden bowl was smooth, entirely rounded beneath, with no flattening at its base; her hands held its fullness.

"Thank you," she said again, lowering the bowl at last.

"*Afwan*," replied the woman. You are welcome. "I am sorry to offer you no milk," she added. "The animals are all gone."

The tent, woven in a deep brown, wool-like material, was bare of furnishings except for the mat they were seated on and a low-slung type of shelf piled with a few blankets and burlap bags. There was a charred cooking-pot, a tea-tray, and the chipped wooden bowl.

Emory put the bowl down, nestling it into the soft sand. "The water," she said, "it is very good. It is from where?"

"There is an old well, narrow but very deep, that has not dried up yet. *Hok* — out there." Settling the now-sleeping infant into the curve of one arm, the woman used the other to indicate the sea of dunes behind the tent. "*Ilhamdullilah*, there is something for us there. For the rest, we survive by the grace of God."

With an unconscious gesture of reverence, she adjusted her *melafah* over the crown of her head. In the brief movement, Emory saw that the pierce-holes of the woman's ears were empty, preserved only with loops of dirty thread. She has traded away everything, Emory thought. Any jewelry she once had, or rugs, or goods of any value.

Choosing her words with care, she asked, "Has anyone — government people, or anyone else — come to help?"

"If they have come, they have not found us." Weariness glazed the woman's eyes; her expression held no anger, no blame.

The turn of an engine broke onto the stillness. A metallic, choking cough, then dead silence again.

Emory sat there, her thoughts hectic. Couldn't they take the woman and the two children in the bush-taxi? But no, it was already full to bursting. And she was waiting here for her husband, she'd said. Months now.

A sudden anger filled her. How could he have gone, leaving her, leaving them like this? Would he come back? And right now, was there anything that could be done, or said? She stared hard at the edge of the frayed mat and clasped her hands tight in her lap.

The woman shifted the sleeping infant and asked something. To Emory, it sounded like, And you, are you with a tent? "*Winti mitkhayma?*"

Uncertain, Emory replied, "I…don't have a tent, no." She added, "I'm just visiting here, traveling with a friend. I live in a house…well, in a building. In a big city. In America."

"*Amrika?*" The woman considered her with worn astonishment, and the boy's black eyes deepened in their fixity. "*Wellah!*" She shook her head and gazed down at the infant as if expecting it to wake and marvel at this as well. When it didn't, she bounced it gently, looked up again, and said, "*Hada jazira, la?*" That's an island, isn't it?

Emory hesitated. "Big island. Across the ocean."

"*Ba'id ktiir.*"

"*Aywa,*" Emory agreed. "Very far."

"Is there desert?"

"Some. Not like this. Not so…so large."

The woman nodded and shifted the infant once more. After a moment she asked again, "*Winti mitkhayma?*"

Emory shook her head. "I'm sorry. I don't understand."

"*Andak rajul?*"

Ah. "No," said Emory. "No, I do not have a man."

"You live with your parents."

Again Emory shook her head. "My mother is in one place, with my stepfather. I live in a different city." Easier not to go into details. "A very big city."

"*Wellahi!*" Surprise animated the woman's tired features. "And you came here from there. *Gharib.*" The word she used to mean "strange" was the word for "west."

Emory dug in her mind for the words to explain: yes, I came to visit a friend. I came because I was curious. Because I did not want to spend another spring break alone. She balked, not for lack of vocabulary, but because of how trivial it all felt here, now.

Motor-sounds again stirred the air, steadying this time and holding. Over the low thrum came the clear peal of Carmen's voice: "Em — come on!"

Emory stared at the woman. "I'm sorry — I have to go." Her fingers brushed the wooden bowl. "Thank you. Thank you very much for the water, and…"

"*Emory!*"

Half-rising to her knees, she looked over her shoulder in the direction of the invisible taxi, then turned back to the woman. "I wish —"

But the woman said, "We must stay here; we are waiting for my husband. He will come soon, *insh'allah.*"

"*Insh'allah,*" said Emory.

Her hands pressed her empty pockets. She had walked away from the taxi with nothing at all. No water-bottle, not a single coin of Mauritanian currency, not even the notebook in which she'd been scribbling throughout the trip. Nothing of any value or practical use.

"Wait." Still on her knees, she fumbled with the minute clasp of her right earring. She undid that one, then the other: small gold hoops that she'd worn so long they seemed part of her body. "I would like you to have these. Please."

The woman stared at her, uncomprehending at first, then shook her head. "These should go one day to your daughter, *insh'allah*," she said.

"But I —"

"*Em!*"

"I just…it is a way of saying 'thank you.' Please take them."

The bright rings gleamed in the husk of the woman's hand. She regarded them in silence and then looked up. "*Shoukran. Shoukran ktiir.*"

But Emory was retreating, shaking her head. *Afwan*, you're welcome; no, truly, it is I who thank you. Embarrassed not by her gesture, but by its inadequacy.

She made her way, stumbling, back over the honey-colored dune. She heard Carmen call out once more as she re-crossed the stretch where the rippled sand changed color. Her pulse pounded in her ears again, and she stood for a moment uncertain of the direction the voice had come from. Then she spotted the two scraggly bushes between the rocks and retraced her steps from there.

She covered the last rise gasping and suddenly was back at the road. Everyone was climbing into the taxi. Carmen stood beside the open rear door, cap pushed back, hands on hips. "So where've you been?"

"God, I'm so sorry…kept you all waiting…"

"It's all right. As it happens, just after the mechanical breakthrough it turned out to be prayer time, so everyone was busy with that for a while. They're all pretty keen to get going now, though. Hey, here, you must need some water."

"I had something to drink, just…"

"What'd you do out there, dig a well?"

"No, I —"

"That's okay. Catch your breath and tell me in the taxi."

"Really, I'm so sorry…" She glanced at the other passengers. The green-veiled woman settled back in her seat with a muttered "*Ilhamdullilah.*"

Carmen's grin was merry. "Don't worry. I think they all figured you went off to find a nice big dune to crouch behind and got lost on the way back."

Emory tucked herself into the taxi between Carmen and the door, its streaky window stuck permanently half-open. With a rattle of resignation the car moved forward, regained the road, and slowly picked up speed in the direction of Nouakchott. Twisting in her seat to look back, Emory squinted against the hot blast of air that hit her full in the face. She strained for a last sight of the lone peak, but it was hidden again among the silent folds of the dunes.

Biographies

Ony Ratsifandrihamanana is 30 years old. She lives in Madagascar and has a background in law and human rights. She has previously published a short story written in French, entitled "Cher Peter," which won a Young French Language Writer Prize and the Young Reader Prize of the Lycée Pierre d'Aragon, and was published by *Buchet-Chastel* in 2013.

Sean Gill is a writer and filmmaker who won *Michigan Quarterly Review*'s 2020 Lawrence Prize, *Pleiades*' 2019 Gail B. Crump Prize, *The Cincinnati Review*'s 2018 Robert and Adele Schiff Award, and was awarded a 2023 Sozopol Seminars Fellowship in Bulgaria. He has studied with Werner Herzog and Juan Luis Buñuel, documented public defenders for *National Geographic*, and currently video edits for Netflix's *Queer Eye* (for which he has received two Primetime Emmy nominations). Recent work has been published in *The Iowa Review*, *McSweeney's Internet Tendency*, *ZYZZYVA*, and *The Threepenny Review*.

Olivia Strauss is a writer and psychotherapist living in Brooklyn with her partner and cat. She is represented by Jon Cobb of HG Literary.

Faith Shearin's seven books of poetry include: *The Owl Question* (May Swenson Award), *Orpheus*, *Turning* (Dogfish Poetry Prize), *Darwin's Daughter* (SFA University Press), and *Lost Language* (Press 53). She has received awards from Yaddo, The National Endowment for the Arts, and The Fine Arts Work Center in Provincetown. Recent work has been read aloud on *The Writer's Almanac* and included in *American Life in Poetry*. Her essays and short stories have received awards from *The Missouri Review*, *New Ohio Review*, and *Bellevue Literary Review* among others. Her first novel, *Lost River, 1918* was published in 2022 by Leapfrog Press.

Lauren Goodsmith currently coordinates services for humanitarian immigrants living in Maryland. She served as a Peace Corps volunteer in Mauritania, West Africa, subsequently writing and photographing the nonfiction book *The Children of Mauritania: Days in the Desert and by the River Shore* (Carolrhoda Books/Lerner Publications,1993; named a "Notable Children's Trade Book in the Field of Social Studies" by the National Council for Social Studies/Children's Book Council). During the course of her overseas work, Lauren served as technical advisor and lead program trainer on prevention of gender-based violence in conflict-affected settings, including refugee camps in Guinea, Rwanda, and Thailand. She has co-authored research studies and written newspaper and journal articles on issues at the intersection of women's health and human rights. Lauren is founder and director of the Intercultural Counseling Connection, a non-profit program based in Baltimore that provides pro bono therapy for forced migrant survivors of torture and trauma.

Contest Finalists

Author   *Manuscript Title*

Author	Manuscript Title
Melanie Bush	Money Makes It Clean
Latifa Ayad	The Realm Unknown
Jonathan Stone	The Secret to Life
Mimi Drop	Mother Earth
Michael Farina	The Last Thing I Did
Nicole Beck	Stream Skin
Natasha Fevre	Chwarel Bay
Tristra Yeager	Starfall
Laura E. Bailey	Hazardous Terrain
Mary Bonina	My Way Home
Katie Harms	Sunny Runs
Yance Wyatt	The Moonshiner's Manual
Seamus Boshell	The Great Wall of Ballygall
Kyla-Yen Giffin	Cosmogon
Steve Lemley	St. Charlene of Meagher, Missouri

Congratulations to the winners and finalists, and our deepest appreciation for all who entered—the decision-making process was extremely difficult at every stage.

www.ingramcontent.com/pod-product-compliance
Lightning Source LLC
LaVergne TN
LVHW041712060526
838201LV00043B/704